"Are you tense ar

Luke inquired gu

When he'd started the

relaxed all over. Now l

"I think you've done enough," she gasped.

"Have I?" His breath laved the shell of her ear as his hands moved to her bared waist. The crop top gave him free access to her abs and he worked on them, slowing his upward progress just beneath her breasts.

"Shall I stop now?" Luke whispered.

"No." Helen moaned and leaned back against him, aware of his pressing erection. Her breasts now filled his hands, his thumbs caressing her nipples through the thin silk top. She imagined Luke touching her everywhere with the same intimacy. She imagined her body vibrating like a fine instrument being tuned.

As if Luke could read her mind, he slid one of his hands slowly downward. "Tell me when to stop."

Helen gasped with pleasure, and the next minute he had turned her slightly and taken her mouth. Mindlessly she kissed him and drew his tongue deeper as he continued to stroke her intimately. She was helpless to fight going over the edge. Moments later she shuddered.

Luke wrapped his arms around her, nuzzled the side of her neck and supported her boneless body, murmuring, "Now you're relaxed...."

Dear Reader,

Chicago is my hometown, and I love exploring diverse neighborhoods and figuring out new ways to put my lovers in danger. Years ago I discovered the Wicker Park/Bucktown area, now an eclectic neighborhood of young professionals, artists, students and others—and what used to be called the "Polish Gold Coast."

What a rich arena for my romantic suspense stories! I used the neighborhood in *Hot Zone,* as well as the previous CHICAGO HEAT books, and happily Harlequin Intrigue's CLUB UNDERCOVER settled into its new home there this spring with *Fake I.D. Wife* and *VIP Protector,* and will continue there in the future.

If you enjoy your CHICAGO HEAT excursion, let me know at Patricia@PatriciaRosemoor.com—or if you prefer snail mail, Patricia Rosemoor, P.O. Box 578297, Chicago, IL 60657-8297. And you can see what's coming up at www.PatriciaRosemoor.com.

Enjoy!

Patricia Rosemoor

Books by Patricia Rosemoor

HARLEQUIN BLAZE

35—SHEER PLEASURE*
55—IMPROPER CONDUCT*

*Chicago Heat miniseries

HOT ZONE

Patricia Rosemoor

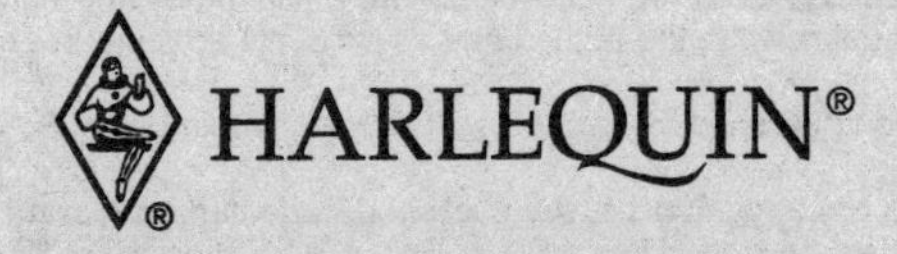

TORONTO • NEW YORK • LONDON
AMSTERDAM • PARIS • SYDNEY • HAMBURG
STOCKHOLM • ATHENS • TOKYO • MILAN • MADRID
PRAGUE • WARSAW • BUDAPEST • AUCKLAND

ISBN 0-373-79099-6

HOT ZONE

This edition published by arrangement with Harlequin Books S.A.

Visit us at www.eHarlequin.com

Printed in U.S.A.

1

"WE DON'T WANT YOU HERE...so go away...and *don't* come back some other day!"

Helen Rhodes led the cheer and the march in front of the pale green tile facade of the building, which had recently been restored to its former glory. Several other small business owners and a handful of neighbors were picketing with her—all of them concerned the neighborhood's flavor would be ruined by a big flashy establishment like this one promised to be. The old Polish Baths had been closed down for years and—unless she stopped it from happening—would be reincarnated into Hot Zone, a superthemed coffeehouse and singles meet-and-greet venue that would put her out of business in short order.

"If you ask me," her friend Annie said over the rumble of the rapid transit train passing nearby, "Helen's Cybercafé is so solid—and so different from this place—it can stand on its own." The expression in the gray eyes behind the frameless glasses looked utterly sincere.

"From your lips," Helen mumbled. But having given up so much in the way of financial security to be her own boss, she wasn't mollified. "Combining coffee with relaxing massages and sexy hot tubs—how brilliant is that?''

''That it is,'' Annie admitted, ''but while Luke DeVries will give them a place to relax, you'll give them a place to work. Different strokes and all that. Just like you and me.''

Grinning down at Annie, Helen hugged her friend and affectionately yanked her ponytail. Despite the August heat wave that had rivulets of sweat running down her own back, Annie was hiding in black leggings and an oversize cotton T-shirt. Nothing at all like her own magenta calf-length pants and orange top, cropped to show off the time she spent in the gym.

''You and I might get along with our shops side by side, but we're friends *and* we don't have competing businesses,'' Helen observed.

''Well, then...'' Annie said, then raised her voice to shout, ''We don't want you here...so go away...and *don't* come back some other day!''

She was nothing if not loyal, Helen thought, joining the chant.

As sweat-drenched workers went in and out of the building, they glared at the people in the picket line.

The eclectic group was representative of a neighborhood in transition, but at this point the businesses were all small and privately owned, and everyone was afraid of having that balance upset. Part of a national chain, this Hot Zone threatened them all. The nearby six-corner area where Milwaukee, Damen and North Avenues intersected and Wicker Park and Bucktown bumped up against each other boasted intimate restaurants, a performance and dance club that was building a name, boutiques that sold funky clothing and accessories, and unique stores that carried comic books and horror memorabilia. The most conservative of the picketers wore business gear—jacket off, tie loosened—the least conservative wore more jewelry than actual clothing.

Whatever the workers thought of the mix, not one of them said a word.

"You would think someone would object, would try to get us to disperse."

"So Nick can get it on video," Annie said knowingly.

Helen was aware that Annie didn't really want to be here—her friend had been on the receiving end of a picket line when she'd first opened her risqué shop, Annie's Attic, now possibly the most popular non-franchised lingerie store in the city. But Annie Wilder and Nick Novak had been her best buddies since college days, so they were both here for her.

Helen looked toward the man behind the camera at the curb and he grinned at her, then gave her a thumbs-up. Nick used to shoot news clips for a local station. And though he now owned his own fledgling video business, she figured with his old contacts, he might be able to get them on tonight's broadcast, assuming it was a slow news night.

Assuming anything interesting ever happened... like the money-grubbing owner coming out of the building to face her!

''Luke DeVries is a coward,'' she muttered, then realized she was addressing the air—Annie had fallen back to talk to Nick.

Starting up the chant once more, Helen shifted the Just Cool It, Hot Zone sign she was carrying to a more comfortable position.

''That getting too heavy?'' came a low-timbered voice.

''A little,'' she said, turning to face the man who was now marching alongside her.

For a moment, Helen felt stunned by the dark-eyed hunk who'd taken Annie's place. Spiked gold-tipped brown hair topped a broad forehead, high cheekbones and a strong chin. When he smiled at her, his left cheek was licked by a sexy dimple.

And Helen nearly dropped her sign.

''Can I carry that for a while?'' he asked.

''Uh, sure.''

As he wrapped his hand around the wooden pole, his fingers grazed hers. Helen gasped, then covered with a cough.

''Summer cold?''

''Allergies. Chicago summers are a bear to get through.''

''I've heard that.''

''You're not from around here,'' she guessed, both from his comment and a hint of southern accent.

''I am now. Beautiful city. Even more beautiful women.''

He was staring at her in a way that heated her blood.

''Do you live close by?'' Helen asked. It was nearly noon, and plenty of people were out for lunch, which was the reason she'd chosen this time to stage her protest. She realized he could be taking a lunch break, so she added, ''Or is your office in the neighborhood?''

''Yes. And yes. So why are we picketing?''

''Because whenever a Hot Zone pops up in a new neighborhood, similar businesses get killed.''

''Killed? Isn't that overly dramatic.''

Helen sighed. He wasn't the first to accuse her of blowing things out of proportion. ''Well, fail, then.''

''But that's competition, the nature of business.''

''If you had your *own* business—''

''I do. And I think as long as a man runs his business ethically—''

''Well, Luke DeVries doesn't. He's a shark in man's clothing.''

He arched a brow at her, triggering her pulse. His face was all planes and angles, cover-model handsome. No man should be this good-looking, Helen thought. Or have such long eyelashes. Thinking maybe he *was* a model...or gay...she squinted at him to make sure the lashes weren't enhanced by additions or mascara. Nope, real.

''So, what's this DeVries character done?'' he asked.

''Nothing to me, at least not yet,'' she admitted. ''I own Helen's Cybercafé, his closest competition, and last time a Hot Zone opened up—in Boston—one of its competitors burned to the ground. There's been plenty of speculation about Hot Zone's involvement."

"Arson?"

"An electrical fire—the investigators couldn't prove anything."

"But you're holding it against him anyway?"

Wondering why he'd joined the picket line—just to argue?—she said, "A woman has to look out for herself."

"She surely does," he agreed. "And in your case, I'd like to help. Maybe we can discuss your situation over dinner."

Aha! It wasn't the *cause* that had caught his interest. "You mean a date?"

"Is that such a surprise?" he asked with a drawl. "I find it hard to believe you don't get dinner offers all the time."

He gave her a languid smile that sent a like feeling from her limbs to her middle. Helen tried not to shudder in reaction, not wanting to give him the advantage.

Alarmed at her instant reaction, she said, "Um, it was just a bit unexpected."

The smile continued to hover about his lips. "So are we on?"

"I don't even know you."

"Isn't that what a date is for—to get to know a person better?"

"That's what *coffee* is for." Irony had always been her strong suit.

"Dinner. Coffee. Whatever you want."

His voice was so low and sexy it made her think of lots of things she might want to do with this man.

"So how about it?" he prodded.

Helen was tempted. Surely, she was. Her basic instincts hadn't been satisfied in months. But this was happening too fast. She was *too* attracted, which in her mind spelled trouble with a capital *T*. She liked having the upper hand in a relationship for the short time it would last, difficult to do if she didn't feel absolutely in control.

"You wouldn't want to go out with me," she said. "I have rules for dating—"

"Rules?" His eyes teased her.

"Actually I only have one rule, a really simple—"

Before she could say *rule* again, he interrupted. "You can tell me about it over dinner. Or coffee. Your choice."

He certainly was insistent. Cocksure as a matter of fact. Then again, with his looks, why wouldn't he be? He probably scored big-time when he put on the charm. Which should be putting her *off* big-time.

Instead, she found herself breathless at the thought of getting to know the man more intimately. And then she found herself asking, "When?"

"Tonight. Seven-thirty."

"I work until...I suppose I could leave early."

That's why she'd finally hired an assistant manager, so she could have time off. Besides, she could handle herself with *any* man, even one so attractive, Helen assured herself. She'd come up with her three-date rule as emotional protection, and she'd never,

ever broken it. And as long as she kept to that, she could have her physical pleasure and keep her psychological health, too.

"Pick me up at the cybercafé," she finally said. "That's at the corner of North and—"

"I know where it is."

Suddenly, she realized they hadn't introduced themselves. "Um, I'm Helen Rhodes."

"Nice to meet you, Helen." Trouble extended his hand and she slipped her beringed fingers in for a shake so that they were stuck there, caught in his strong fingers, when he said, "Luke. Luke DeVries."

Helen gasped. For a moment her fingers went boneless and she felt utterly trapped. The shark himself had her in his jaws! Then she jerked her hand from his and made a fist to stop herself from smacking him for tricking her so basely.

"What is this? Some stupid juvenile prank?"

He was already moving away from her, toward the entrance of the former baths. "No joke," he said. "Seven-thirty. Be hungry."

"I changed my mind!" she shouted after him, but he'd already disappeared inside.

"Changed your mind about what?" Annie asked, coming up alongside her. "And who was the hunk?"

Knowing Luke DeVries wouldn't be so easily put off, Helen muttered, "Trouble. Big, *big* trouble."

LUKE ENTERED the air-conditioned baths but found it hard to cool down with Helen Rhodes still vivid in his mind.

What a knockout! Golden blonde curls, just a hint of tan kissing her creamy skin all dewy with perspiration, eyes like emeralds and a bombshell body. That tempting bared stomach with its pierced navel intrigued him, made him want to run his tongue along the exposed flesh until it quivered and she gasped with pleasure. The primal image stirred his own flesh. He would look forward to pursuing the woman while he was based in Chicago.

Too bad she wanted to run him out of town on a rail…or maybe it wasn't. A duel of wits with her would make the challenge more interesting, that was for certain.

Grinning at the thought, Luke had no doubts he could change Helen's mind about stepping out with him.

Women liked him, and he genuinely liked them, even if he wasn't into relationships. How could he be when he was building a business that took him from city to city? He couldn't let anyone depend on him any more than he could depend on them. Life with his military career dad had taught him how fleeting personal relationships were, so he simply didn't try to create them.

But whether in business or in private pursuits, his persuasive powers were legend. Maybe he did have a bit of the shark in him. He wouldn't hesitate to turn on the charm to high gear to get what he wanted. And he was certain that if he did this time, he could loosen Helen up, get her to listen to reason, keep her off his back business-wise—and if he was really lucky, enjoy her on a more intimate level.

In the meantime, he had work to do, the interior of the baths being in the final stages of transformation.

He caught the eye of Alexis Stark, his personal assistant, and waved her over. Five feet of raw energy, she practically flew to his side, blue-tipped strands of unevenly cut dark hair waggling like mini-antennae.

"Hey, boss, what's up?"

"Special assignment."

She opened her notepad, apparently ready to write down his instructions. "How special?"

"One that'll get the wolf from our door."

Alexis furrowed her brow. "Wolf? Is that literal, or are we in financial trouble?"

"I mean the picketers. Well actually, their leader, Helen Rhodes."

"Gonna have her arrested?"

"Gonna charm her into submission."

"Submission, hmm." Her blue-lined eyes widened. "How come you never make *me* an offer like that?"

Luke laughed. Her comment blatantly sexual, he assumed she made love the way she did everything—full blast. Though he'd never been attracted to Alexis, he didn't want to hurt her feelings, so he said, "Because you work for me. It wouldn't be ethical." Which was true enough.

Alexis looked as if she had a comeback, but then thought better of it and swallowed whatever she meant to say. He caught an odd expression flitting through her eyes before she lowered them to the pad of paper and pen.

"Okay," she said, her smile appearing a bit forced. "So what's the plan?"

Luke gave her a quick summary of his basic idea and left the details to her. "Do that thing you do so well."

Again, the strained expression. "Got it, boss."

Then Luke turned his attention to the job at hand.

For the next hour, he focused on the workmen. On the small details that put his personal stamp on every Hot Zone, this being number thirteen. Lucky thirteen, he thought proudly, and the fifth city in three years.

Halfway through the afternoon, he'd just approved the paint color for the entryway—a deep, pulsing red with a hint of blue—when his public relations director wove toward him. In three-and-a-half-inch heels, she topped six feet, bringing them nearly nose to nose.

"A coup," the redhead said in way of greeting. "Maybe I should change my name to Coup Gordon."

Luke smiled at her whimsy. "Leave well enough alone—'Flash' says it all. So what's up?"

Florence "Flash" Gordon gave him one of her famous hundred-watt smiles, the obvious source of the nickname she'd adopted, Flash being far more memorable than Florence for a woman in public relations.

"A source told me you were going to be on the ten o'clock news!" she announced gleefully.

"And this is a good thing?"

He wasn't thrilled with the last media coverage he'd gotten, when that neighboring café went up in flames. Not that Flash had been at fault. Knowing her, she'd probably contained the story. Things certainly could have gotten worse.

"This is a triumph," she said. "That guy who was shooting the video of the picket line? He sold a local station on running footage...and I happen to know the news anchor. Personally. *Very* personally."

"So you got it pulled."

"And miss an opportunity to herald in the opening of Hot Zone? Not on your life! I simply got him to show me the footage so I could help him pick what to use...and what to add to the commentary. Trust me on this one, Luke. Gotta go. Things to do, people to entice. Ta!"

Flash headed for the stairs and the temporary second-floor offices, set up for their use while they were in Chicago.

Luke had no reason to doubt Flash. She was an expert at putting out fires. So why did a frisson of unease follow him as he got back to work? Undoubtedly, the clip wouldn't go the way Helen had planned, which would make her one unhappy lady. Good thing it wouldn't air until after their evening together. Or perhaps they'd be otherwise occupied into the wee hours of the morning....

Not that he would regret anything if it meant protecting his growing coffeehouse empire.

He'd come far from his raw beginnings, probably because he put every fiber of his being into his business.

And every ounce of savvy and charm.

Whatever it took.

HELEN WAS STILL STEAMING as zero hour drew closer. She was working at one of the café's computers, building a Web site for a new freelance client, when Kate Malone, her assistant manager, stopped to look over her shoulder.

"What do you think?" Helen asked, pointing to the jazzy set of buttons and bars on the screen.

"I think you should be getting ready instead of working. I thought you hired me so you could have some free time."

Helen glanced up at Kate with her short white-blonde hair and retro horn-rimmed glasses. The young woman was too thin and so pale she looked like a wraith, someone who could simply disappear in a crowd.

"Unfortunately, time spent with Luke DeVries wouldn't be free," Helen muttered. Quickly, she saved the graphics set. "I'd be paying a big price."

"I don't get it."

"Never mind."

Helen didn't know Kate well enough to confide in her—she'd only hired the other woman some weeks before. And her best friends weren't available to lend their ears. Unfortunately she'd seen Annie climb on the back of Nate's motorcycle and ride off with him. And Nick had said he was taking his girlfriend Isabel and her sister Louise to an early movie. So she had no one to gripe to but herself.

Or maybe her time would be better spent figuring out a maneuver that would pay off. That's what Luke DeVries was doing, she was certain. He hadn't gotten into the picket line next to her without knowing who she was. He'd tricked her, had gotten her interested, then gone in for the kill—not that she wouldn't have seen through him given a few more moments.

Turn around was fair play, she mused. So he thought he could use her, charm her into seeing things his way.... Well, let him underestimate her.

He would be in for a big surprise.

She reopened the page she'd been working on. The Web site was for Muscle Beach, a new workout facility located on a beach overlooking Lake Michigan. This was the second of its sort, the one at North Avenue Beach so successful that another gym had been opened farther north. But their Web site had been created too quickly and with little panache. Helen had put in her bid to fix that and had easily won the contract.

But this was a bad time to be working on something that took such concentration, she thought, trying not to look too closely at the provided photos, many of which were gorgeous young men showing off their oil-slicked musculature.

Gorgeous musculature that reminded her of Luke DeVries's body.

Though he'd been fully dressed in trousers and a knit polo shirt, she hadn't missed the breadth of his shoulders or the expanse of his chest or the trimness of his waistline. Imagining him in nothing but a scrap of swimwear made her pulse rush, and she realized she would love to see him like that...or in nothing at all.

Flustered, hoping Kate wouldn't notice the flush she felt warm her cheeks, Helen quickly finished adding buttons to the page, saved her work and copied it to disk before taking herself off to the rest room. There she touched up her makeup and finger-combed her wild curls. Most women with naturally curly hair tried to straighten it—often in vain—but Helen worked with what she had to her best advantage.

Just as she would with Luke DeVries, she mused, thinking she would get a grip on herself and remember why she was going through with this charade. She returned to the café and looked at its crackled yellow walls, row of computers and upholstered couch and chairs around the fireplace. She'd seen to every detail, picked every chair and every decorative item herself.

She even knew her regular customers by name and knew what they drank. Books stacked next to one of the computers, Sam the student was hard at work. He drank his coffee strong and black. Laura the housewife and mother parked her toddler Jenny on one of the couches. The little girl slurped chocolate milk while Laura drank a mochachino. And Tilda, the old homeless woman, sat in a corner window with her plastic bags and watched the world go by as she poured more sugar into her decaf. Somehow, Helen had gotten attached to them and her other regulars, as well—people who'd found a second home here.

None of whom fit the Hot Zone profile, so where would they go if Helen's Cybercafé ceased to exist?

Her baby was in jeopardy.

The entry door opened and in walked Annie, jiggling a bag. ''Hey.''

''I thought you and Nate were off somewhere.''

''He just took me to the drugstore. Got some photos developed.'' She dropped the bag down on a table and sat. ''I came back to show you.''

''Hah! You came back to see what I would do when Luke DeVries walked through that door.''

Annie grinned and a dimple puckered her cheek. ''You know me too well.''

Helen checked the clock. ''Fifteen minutes more, assuming he's punctual. Kate, could you please get us a couple of cappuccinos?''

''Sure thing.''

While getting jazzed just thinking about Luke, Helen attentively looked over the photographs. She couldn't deny the twinge of envy she felt. The photos were mostly of Annie and Nate. Together. A real couple who would someday be man and wife. Not that she resented their happiness. Or Nick's with Isabel, for that matter. Her two best friends being attached and her having no one simply changed the dynamics a bit.

Her being the fifth wheel didn't change how the three friends felt about each other, she assured herself. They would always be there for one another.

''So what are your plans for tonight?'' Annie asked, stacking the photos in a neat pile.

''What do you mean?''

''Don't give me that innocent face. I know you

better than that. You always think the worst of men, just like you did about Nate. The things you said about him are nothing compared to your comments about Luke DeVries. So why are you going out with him? I mean, I'd like to say, great, go for it, but I know you, Helen. You compartmentalize everything, including your heart."

"All right, so I'm looking out for myself. I'm going to get to know Luke DeVries better so that I can find his Achilles' heel," Helen said, ignoring the way her heart beat a bit faster at the thought of being alone with the man.

"That's not like you."

"I don't care. I want leverage. I don't intend to let him put me out of business. How do I know he hasn't already started his campaign to ruin me?" Helen asked. "If I hadn't caught it last week, that carton of spoiled chicken salad could have sent several of my customers to the emergency room. And, before that, I had the electrical problem that shut me down for a day and a half."

"Which Nate assured you was simply a glitch in the system," Annie reminded her.

Nate was not only Annie's fiancé but their commercial landlord, as well.

"Whatever," Helen muttered.

"Maybe you ought to give the guy a break," Annie told her. "Take a wait-and-see attitude."

"If I wait and see and find I'm right, it'll be too late for this business."

Kate delivered the cappuccinos. "All businesses

have problems of various sorts. So a couple of cafés closed when a Hot Zone opened nearby. Could be nothing more than coincidence. And are you sure it's all true...or is some of that rumor generated by bored busybodies?"

"She has a point," Annie said.

"I can only hope so."

Before they could further discuss the issue, Luke DeVries himself walked through the door.

Though still dressed casually, he had changed clothing. Helen squirmed a little since she was still wearing the same calf-length pants and crop top she'd donned that morning. She hadn't had a chance to get home, shower and change. But he certainly had.

His tan trousers were perfectly pleated and his soft gold polo shirt set off his tan and picked up the highlights in his freshly spiked hair. He set his hands in his pockets as he looked around approvingly, and Helen noted he wore a gold Rolex on one wrist and a gold linked bracelet on the other.

GQ, she thought as his dark gaze finally found hers. Definitely *GQ.*

And if she wanted him for the evening, he was all hers....

For a moment—for one heart-stopping moment—Helen forgot every objection she had about the man.

2

LUKE TOOK ONE LOOK at their faces and knew Helen had been talking about him to her friend and the pale employee who whipped around and headed back behind the counter.

"Did I interrupt something?"

"We were just chatting," Helen said, her long magenta fingernails tapping against a mug. "Passing the time until you arrived."

"Uh-huh. Well, I'm here now, darlin'." Luke gave her his widest grin. "And you're ready to go?"

From the expression that crossed Helen's stunning features, Luke figured he'd been right to wonder if he would have to sweet-talk her. But in the end, she got to her feet and he realized she'd sweet-talked herself into an evening with him. He could tell she was anxious to get out the door. Afraid she might change her mind?

He looked past her to her friend still seated and politely held out his hand. "Luke DeVries."

Giving him a no-nonsense shake and a once-over that would intimidate a lesser man, the woman said, "Annie Wilder."

Luke inclined his head. "Annie's Attic. I've heard

nothing but praise for the way you handle your business. And that display window of yours is a real eye pleaser."

Behind her glasses, Annie's eyes blinked and took on a new shine. "Well...thanks."

Helen cleared her throat. "So are we going somewhere or what?"

Luke turned his grin on her. "I guess we are."

She opened the door before he could get to it, but he took it from her and placed a light hand on her back. On her bare back. She hadn't changed her outfit and her midriff was still exposed. Her skin seemed to come alive under his hand. *He* came alive and took a deep breath to steady himself.

"What are you driving?" Out at the curb, she looked around for a vehicle.

"I thought the walk would do us good," he said, taking her elbow and hurrying her across the busy intersection. "You know...stretch the muscles...relax."

"We need to relax?"

"*You* certainly do, darlin'. You're wound up tighter than a diamondback rattler."

She flexed and subtly freed her arm as they walked up Milwaukee Avenue. "You're comparing me to a snake?"

"Why, snakes can be right sexy."

"Uh-huh."

"I'm serious. Ever touched one?"

"No."

"They're long and firm and smooth to the touch. And when you hold one in your hand—"

"I don't care to hold one..." Her voice trailed off and her expression turned suspicious. "We are still talking about snakes, aren't we?"

"You tell me," Luke said, laughing.

Helen laughed, too, though she tried to cover and it came out more like a snort. She didn't seem to mind, though. At least she had a sense of humor.

He congratulated himself. The ploy had worked. While his beautiful nemesis probably wasn't totally relaxed, she did seem a bit more at ease with him.

Which lasted only a moment before she asked, "So what is this really about, Mr. DeVries?"

"Call me Luke. What do you mean 'this'?"

"Dinner. Coffee. Whatever."

"Simple. I thought if we spent some quality time together, you could get to know me and my business better and realize I'm no threat to you."

"That's to be seen," she muttered, and he wasn't certain she was referring to their businesses.

And then her gaze seemed to fix on the building ahead and her spine seemed to lengthen and she seemed to grow an inch. She gave him an intent look.

"Hot Zone? That's where you're planning on taking me?"

"How else can you see how the work is coming along?" he asked, unlocking the door and smoothly ushering her inside.

Helen started. The click of the lock behind her

sounded so...final. Her heart fluttered and she could hear the rush of her pulse through her ears.

What was wrong with her? Of course Luke would lock the place up for safety's sake. And if he had other ideas, so what? She certainly didn't have to go along with them.

But she certainly had been going along with him to this point. And she continued to do so by following him from the red-hot foyer into the golden-walled main room with windows to the street on one side and a glass-block wall on the alley side.

"Have a look around," Luke said.

Helen was already looking. She noted an alcove on the far side of the spacious room with steps up to a gigantic hot tub. Two doorways led to locker rooms, if the Ladies and Gents signs were any indication. Past the locker rooms, she noted another alcove with a steam room and sauna.

Seating for the coffeehouse itself was split between three levels, the top level being where they'd come in. Helen stepped forward and peered down to the lower levels with their mosaic tiled walls in blues and greens and golds. The groupings of white-wicker sofas and chairs on the middle level had cushions of gold and red with touches of blue and green to connect with the tile.

"This used to be the swimming pool and the tile is original," Luke told her, so close behind her that his breath ruffled her hair and tickled the back of her ear. "What do you think?"

Sensation rushing through her, Helen thought she

wanted to have sex with him right then and there on one of the exotic print couches. The effect he was going for, she was certain. Hot Zone was meant for seduction. She turned to face him, subtly giving herself some breathing space.

"Do you rent rooms upstairs?"

He laughed at her sarcasm. "Sorry, I'm not running a brothel."

"Could have fooled me."

"So you don't like it?"

"It's well executed," she admitted, not wanting to get too enthusiastic about her competition. "And you're going to pay for all this selling coffee?"

"And light fare and desserts...back massages and spa passes on the weekends."

"So you've done this before."

"Nope. Every Hot Zone offers something different. The one in Hollywood is in an old movie theater, for example. And one in Santa Fe is also an art gallery. We offer programs and craft demonstrations along with refreshments. Speaking of which...dinner or coffee? What's your pleasure? We intend to induce a lot of pleasure around here."

He heard her breath catch in her throat. She was trying to hide her reaction but the tiny sound was so revealing.

He also saw it in her face—her features softening like a woman contemplating being satiated in every way. And he saw it in her gemstone eyes, emeralds that shone with depth. For the first time, he noted the tiny mole at the corner of her right eye.

Fascinated, he couldn't help but stare.

Her stomach growled, breaking the intimate moment. "Um, dinner, please," she finally said with a shrug and added, "You said to be hungry."

"Do you usually follow orders?"

"Only if the whim takes me."

He stepped closer and was a little surprised when she stayed put—they were almost touching. "Now, why don't I get the feeling that you're a whimsical sort of a girl?"

"Woman. So what kind am I?"

"Pragmatic…opinionated…stubborn…"

"Be still my heart. If you're not careful, Luke DeVries, you'll turn my head."

Knowing this was his cue to say something equally witty, Luke went straight for the truth instead. "You didn't let me finish. I meant to add exceedingly beautiful."

Then she took a step back and the sparkle in her eyes dissipated. A moment ago, she was interested. Now she was wary. Because he'd told her she was beautiful? How odd.

"So, where are we off to?" she asked.

"Your choice." And as she headed for the foyer, he said, "Pick a table. Any table."

"Here?"

"That's the plan."

He simply wondered how much of his plan she would be willing to go along with.

DEFINITELY IMPRESSED with Luke's plans for this Hot Zone, Helen tried not to show it. The man was too confident...too full of himself...too tempting. Thus, the reason she'd chosen a table on the top seating level. Below, those couches looked sinfully comfortable and she didn't want to let down her guard. An opportunist, Luke DeVries would pounce on any weakness, she was certain...definitely he would pounce on her.

Her skin sizzled at the thought and she squirmed in her chair and told herself to behave.

But warnings didn't help under the glow of fine wine and seductive company. She had grown too mellow for words. Too comfortable to be sharp-witted. Truth be told, she was enjoying herself more than she had in...well, maybe ever.

When Luke brought out a heavily laden tray from the kitchen, she practically salivated over the luscious-looking food. And over the luscious-looking man.

The overheads were dimmed, a single candle was lit and so was she as he set down the tray, placed a tiny baked brie surrounded by grapes between them and slid into the chair opposite her.

"So tell me about this rule of yours," Luke said, refilling her wineglass.

"Three dates."

"Three dates and then what?"

"And then nothing. I go on with my life."

"On to the next man."

"If one appeals to me, yes." *He* appealed to her, but that didn't mean she was going to do anything about it.

She only dated men she was drawn to physically. He thought the three-date rule meant three strikes and a guy was out, while in her mind it meant three steps to sexual satisfaction. Of course, if there was no sizzle in the first place, physical contact wasn't an option at all…not that she always acted on the attraction anyway. If a guy looked like an Adonis but acted like a jerk, no amount of sizzle would move her.

But truth be told, she had needs and, unlike Annie, wasn't willing to go without sex for years until Mr. Right came along…assuming that ever happened. She'd simply resolved to ensure the dating experience suited her needs.

"How curious," Luke said. "I would love to hear the reasoning behind your dating rule."

"I'll bet you would."

Ignoring the sizzle she felt now, Helen took a bite of the brie in flaky pastry and let the warmed cheese melt in her mouth so she wouldn't say anything she would regret.

No way would she tell him about the series of college guys who'd wanted her for a trophy girlfriend. Who'd subsequently dumped her for some nice, safe girl that the guy could bring home to mom. She'd been too wild, too honest and open about her feelings, too willing to give a guy her all, especially her heart, only to have it all thrown back at her. Guys had never considered her serious girlfriend material simply because she was *too* good-looking.

She wouldn't have believed it if one of her exes

hadn't put it on the line for her. He'd told her that he couldn't handle that men would always buzz around her because of her looks and, with so much temptation, he simply couldn't trust her not to stray.

After having her heart broken too many times, she'd decided that she needed to protect herself from further hurt.

She didn't want to end up like her mother.

"So the question is...do you consider this a date?" Luke asked. "Or is it simply a fact-finding mission?"

"What?"

"Ah, such innocence." He saluted her and took a bite of cheese, then washed it down with wine.

"I don't know what this is," she protested truthfully.

Though he'd guessed her original intention, she was admittedly intrigued by Luke DeVries. He stimulated her in every way possible...but no, she couldn't let herself go wild with him. He was her nemesis. He was the shark who could put her out of business.

Might purposely *drive* her out of business.

And yet...

He didn't seem like the type of man who had to play dirty to get what he wanted. His concept for a winning business was brilliant. Not only this Hot Zone, but the others that she'd read about and he'd mentioned, as well.

As impressed as she was by his unique coffeehouse concept, she was even more impressed by the man himself. She'd always been drawn to creative, talented people, Annie and Nick being prime examples. Luke was right up there, right at the top of the list.

''Since you're so hung up on those rules of yours, I don't think we should consider this a date,'' he said.

''Really. And why is that?''

''Because then maybe you can relax.''

Helen laughed. ''No problem. I couldn't be more relaxed.''

Yeah, right, like that was really possible with him sitting there, looking good enough to eat. Trying to turn herself off, she pressed her thighs together.

Though she could see by his expression that he thought she was lying, he said, ''Good. More wine?''

''I think this is where the serious food part comes in.''

Until now they'd merely nibbled on cheese and grapes. Helen's mouth watered as Luke took the two plates of lobster salad from the tray and set them on the table, adding a basket of fresh croissants and butter between.

She dug in before asking, ''So what did you do before serving up sex with coffee?''

Luke arched a brow at her phrasing. ''I worked for Cooper Coffee Company. I was traveling to places like Mexico and Costa Rica and Guatemala to find new organic beans for the company,'' he said, then turned the conversation back on her. ''What made you decide to open your own business?''

''Burnout. Being a corporate Web mistress is a full-time job. And I really mean full-time. Sometimes eighty hours a week. I figured if I wasn't going to have much of a personal life, I might as well be working for myself instead of someone else.''

''Corporate Web mistress? You were kind of young for that much responsibility, weren't you?''

''An industry baby, yes, but computers always interested me, from the time I was a kid.''

''So what was the final straw that made you give up a regular paycheck?''

''More like a challenge by the name of Nick Novak. He was the guy shooting footage of the protest this morning.''

''Aha,'' he said knowingly.

''No 'aha' about it. Nick and Annie and I have been best buddies since college. All three of us were working too hard and were disillusioned about ever having a real life again. No downtime and we weren't even working for ourselves,'' she said, remembering how unhappy she'd become at her job. ''When Cornerstone Realty renovated the six-corners building, Nick jumped at the chance to rent space and start his own business. And he dared Annie and me to jump with him. And we did.'' Realizing she was telling him more than she wanted to, Helen quickly shifted the topic to the cuisine. ''This lobster is divine, by the way.''

''Only the best for a beauti—woman like you,'' he finished. ''But why a coffeehouse?''

Helen realized Luke had stopped himself from calling her beautiful. Inwardly she was pleased both that he thought she was *and* that he was sensitive enough to pick up on her earlier reaction. She also realized he was focused when he wanted information, undoubtedly a prime reason for his success.

"The Internet aspect appealed to me," she told him. "And it gave me the chance to take on some freelance Web clients. I build Web sites at one of the café computers when traffic is slow."

"So you're running two businesses?"

"No, just keeping my hand in. I never know when I might have to find a real job again." She looked at him pointedly.

Luke raised his hands in surrender. "Tell me what I can do to assure you that I have no intentions of driving you out of business."

"I'm not sure you can."

"So you don't trust me."

"Should I?"

"Yes."

"Would *you* trust *me* if our roles were reversed?" Helen asked. "Be honest now."

"I would give you the benefit of the doubt, draw my own conclusions about you rather than accepting what other people say."

"Other people? What about the media?"

He gave her a look. "Right, newspeople are always reliable. They can sell papers and TV ads with boring facts. Have you ever noticed how many stories contain the word 'alleged' as if that morally protects them when they go after a story and make it try to sound hot? And then if they find out things weren't quite what they seemed...well, oops. But their asses are covered.''

Helen couldn't help gaping at him. Indignation looked good on him. Great, as a matter of fact. And very, very sexy. His hair practically bristled and his features suddenly appeared more rough-cut and his voice took on a tone that sliced through to her very core.

This Luke really turned her on, Helen realized, squirming in her chair.

The charmer was lovely but aroused her suspicions. A cover, she thought. An act. A way to get people to trust him. *Most* people. Not her, though. She might be physically attracted to the polished Luke DeVries, but—a straight shooter herself—she thought she liked the rough-hewn man a whole lot better.

''Enough pontificating,'' he muttered, digging into his food and hiding his real self once more.

Helen figured there was a story behind his public persona. She only wished she was privy to it. But what did it matter, really? They weren't on a date. They were *both* on fact-finding missions.

Proven by Luke himself when he asked, ''I'm curious as to why you waited so long to stage the protest against Hot Zone in this location. Why not when you first heard about it, rather than right before the opening?''

''I wasn't paying attention,'' she admitted. ''I was preoccupied with a new business, and then my friends had personal problems.'' Dangerous problems, but thankfully they'd come out unscathed. ''By the time

I found out that Hot Zone was opening...'' she shrugged, ''it was a done deal.''

''Then why bother?''

''Hope.''

Hope that, no matter what, her business would survive. The picketing had really come too late, but she hadn't known how else to attack. To protect her interests. Thankfully, Luke didn't press her but let the subject drop.

Dessert was simple—chocolate flan. One taste and Helen was in heaven. But the real treat was the special coffee topped with a dollop of whipped cream that Luke made for them. She took a sniff.

''Chocolate...almond...and...?''

''Coconut. We call it Hot Bliss in the stores, but personally I think of it as an Orgasm.''

Taking a sip, she nearly choked. ''Orgasm?''

''Don't you feel it?'' he asked, his expression suspiciously innocent.

Which had her scoping out Luke even more intently. He seemed attracted to her, so would he make a move? He'd said not to count this as a date, so maybe not. She couldn't help but think about it as she carefully licked her spoon clean and wondered what it would be like to lick him instead.

The thought built an uncomfortable tension as she continued to wonder how this evening would end.

While Luke cleared the table—he refused to let her help him—Helen walked around the spa area, noting the You Must Wear A Swimsuit At All Times warning posted near the hot tub and sauna areas. She raised her eyebrows and wondered how many people would be tempted to ignore the sign.

Two back-massage chairs were set out, ready for clients. She'd had full body massages many times, but never one of these.

Thinking that if her old corporation had provided tension releasers for its employees, she might never have quit, Helen slipped into the seat and leaned forward, her knees, chest and elbows resting on upholstered pads, and imagined having someone work out her physical tension after a long, tiring day.

She closed her eyes a minute and imagined fingers smoothing the back of her neck.

And then they were…

"Uh, Luke?"

"Hmm?"

"What are you doing?"

"Helping you relax."

So was that a line or had he recognized her growing discomfort at dinner?

"Are you licensed?" she asked.

"More like experienced. You have a knot right here."

"Uhhhh." She moaned as he kneaded the area and a mixture of pleasure and pain filled her. "Something to be said for experience."

He worked his way higher, up her neck and into her hairline, then down along her spine. She felt her body puddle under his practiced hands.

And then she felt him move behind her and somehow balance himself on the back of the seat. His hands worked their way from her shoulders down to her elbows. His arms had her surrounded, she thought hazily. And slowly she became aware of the erection pressing into her tush.

Her pulse shot up like a rocket and her eyes were wide open as he murmured, ''Any other tense places you want me to work out?''

A minute ago she'd been relaxed all over. Now her whole body was tight.

''I think you've done enough,'' she gasped.

''Have I?'' His breath laved the shell of her ear and his warmth pressed into her back. ''I'll stop if you want, just say the word.''

He was working on her hands now, thumbs pressing into her palms and, one by one, muscles everywhere let go. Feeling his arms flex against hers, Helen opened her mouth to tell him that he could stop now, but nothing came out.

Date or not, they'd skipped the first stage and proceeded directly to the second.

Luke slid his hands up to her elbows then moved to her bared waist. The crop top gave him free access to her abs, and he worked on them, slowing his upward progress just beneath her breasts.

''Shall I stop now?'' Luke murmured.

Helen moaned and leaned back against him and away from the chest pad. ''No.''

And when he moved higher, she arched so that her breasts filled his hands. His thumbs caressed her already distended nipples through the thin silk covering them. Heaven help her, she was so turned on she'd lost all her good sense.

Helen moaned and her lashes fluttered closed and she imagined Luke touching her everywhere with the same intimacy. She imagined her body vibrating like a fine instrument being tuned.

As if Luke could read her mind, he slid one of his hands slowly downward. "Tell me when to stop."

In response she pressed her tush slightly against his erection. His turn to moan. He pressed back and when she gasped "More!" he plunged the wandering hand into her slacks and found her sweet spot through the already wet silk covering her.

Helen gasped with pleasure, and the next moment he shifted behind her so that he could hook a hand behind her neck and turn her slightly and take her mouth. Mindlessly, she kissed him and drew his tongue deeper as he continued to stroke her below. His finger parted her folds through the material and found her center.

Helen thought it the most erotic sensation she'd ever experienced. Moving against his hard-on, she longed to touch him, as well, but since they were precariously balanced on the equipment, undue movement might prove disastrous. But Luke wasn't complaining. He was pressing into her and she could hear his breathing deepen. Then she felt him harden and lengthen even further through their clothing.

Wanting nothing more than to turn and take his erection into her mouth, she couldn't act on the desire, could only imagine the taste and texture of him.

But the fantasy of it and the repeated pressure of his finger sliding against her clit was enough to make the trembling start deep inside.

"If you don't stop that, I'm going to come," she gasped.

"That's good, isn't it?"

He nipped at the flesh between shoulder and neck and increased the pressure below. Helen was helpless to fight going over the edge. He kissed her again and she came in long waves of pleasure.

When the shuddering stopped, Luke wrapped his arms around her middle, nuzzled the side of her neck and supported her boneless body, murmuring, "Now you're relaxed."

THROUGH NARROWED EYES, she watched them exit Hot Zone. Too absorbed in one another, their bodies practically vibrating with some intensity, they didn't see her standing in the shadows on the other side of the street.

She tried to read their body language, tried to get a hold on what was going on between them. Anger? No, not anger exactly. Attraction? Some combination of both?

For a moment, fury seared her.

After all she'd done for him…how dare he!

No, no, be reasonable, a little voice said. *This is nothing. Meaningless. Doesn't matter in the big scheme of things.*

She took a shaky breath and faced facts. Luke was all man, after all, and until she was in his personal life for good, she would have to expect some slips. That's all this was, she assured herself, following their progress down the street.

She didn't have to worry about Helen Rhodes. His women never lasted in his life, not like she did. She'd been there for him since he'd started Hot Zone.

Before.

He owed everything to her.

All the success. The money. The media.

Everything.

Once he understood that, all would fall into place and her life would be perfect.

3

"I WOULD SAY this counted as a date," Helen stated as they headed away from Hot Zone the way they arrived—on foot.

"How do you get that?" Luke asked, waiting for his hard-on to roll over and play dead. How the hell was that supposed to happen when the cause was bumped up against his side, ripe and apparently ready for anything? "I thought we agreed this was no more than a fact-finding mission."

Why the semantics worried him, he had no clue. Maybe he simply liked arguing with her, which certainly was a perverted kind of turn-on.

"This way," she said, turning up the block when they got to the next corner. "What started as fact-finding ended as sex."

"We didn't have sex," he stated.

"Excuse me?"

"Foreplay doesn't count."

"Orgasms do."

"Unless you count the beverage kind, I didn't have one," he reminded her.

"And that's my fault?"

"No, darlin', I take full credit for that omission."

"So why didn't you..."

"Have my way with you? Because it wasn't a date. I was simply trying to get you to loosen up and things got a tad out of hand. Or *in* hand as the case may be," he said with a chuckle. "That was simply spontaneous combustion...mostly on your part."

Though *he* felt ready to explode. The idea of being inside her was heating his blood, and he figured it was doing the same to Helen. Not that she was being open or obvious about what he was sure she wanted as much as he did. And he planned to give her what she wanted before this night was through. He would have given it to her already—several times if he could credit his imagination—but something had kept him from pushing too far, too fast.

"Is that relaxation technique standard business procedure for you?"

Luke grinned into the night. "Not so far, but I'm thinking of adding it to my repertoire of negotiation skills."

The comment drew a reluctant-sounding chuckle out of Helen, but she seemed to relax a bit.

"So where are you taking me?" he asked.

"Home."

"Sounds promising."

"Rather, you're walking me home since you didn't drive," she clarified.

"I never said I didn't drive. My SUV's parked in back of Hot Zone."

"And I would have guessed you were the sports car type."

"I am, but a sports car isn't too practical when you're getting a new business up and running. The SUV hauls a lot of whatever I need."

"So what is it you need?" she asked as they crossed under a set of elevated rapid-transit tracks.

"That's a loaded question if I ever heard one. Right now I need you. I need to tear off your clothes and taste your flesh and bury myself deep inside you."

He could hear her gasp into the quiet night.

Then, sounding breathless, she asked, "Are you planning on carrying through with that need?"

"I haven't made up my mind. You?"

Helen's clearing her throat sounded suspiciously like a choking noise. "I don't usually talk so frankly about sex with a man."

"I would imagine if you're having sex it's with a man and…then again, if you were having it with a woman—"

"No!"

"—then I would be happy being a fly on your wall."

"Not a chance."

"All right, then!" he said with increasing enthusiasm. "I'll join in. I'm always open to new experiences."

She shook her head in exasperation, then sent a sideways glance his way. "You mean you haven't…"

"Only in my dreams."

Wet ones. Which was bound to happen that night

if he didn't stop joking about sex. Or if he didn't get some relief.

They made another turn, walked to the end of the block and turned again only to stop after several yards before an imposing three-story building with a gray limestone facade set on a huge corner lot surrounded by black iron fencing.

"This is it," she said.

"Your apartment?"

"No, it's a house."

"Roommates?"

She shook her head.

He raised his eyebrows and whistled. "Cybercafés must be more lucrative than I ever imagined."

"My business doesn't pay for the mortgage. My trust fund does."

"Trust fund," he echoed.

"Since I was twenty-one. It's not the same as having a real father in my life, but when it's all a girl has... I was able to save enough for the down payment. I bought the place two years ago, and now the trust fund takes place of the mortgage and taxes. At least if I go out of business I won't be out on the street."

He thought about pursuing the father thing, but he suspected it was a sore point, so instead he said, "Out on the street? Uh-uh, that would never happen to you."

"How do you know?"

"Because type A personalities always have a

backup plan. The Web sites you're building,'' he reminded her.

Her renewed laughter sounded lovely. Almost as lovely as she herself was.

Streetlight filtered through the trees, just enough that he could see exactly how lovely. Stunning, really. Eyes wide, she stared back at him.

He dipped his head to taste her mouth. Just her mouth, nothing more. Something made him want to go slowly with her. As he kissed her, a pulse seemed to beat through the night, but he realized it was his own heartbeat rushing through his head.

The kiss ended with a collective gasp. The tension was so thick...

''I've been thinking,'' he said, trying to distract himself. Trying to find a reason to see her again that couldn't be called a date. For some reason, he didn't want her to start counting the dates he had with her. ''I could use new blood working on my Web site.''

Her soft expression hardened. ''What? You aren't trying to bribe me, are you?''

''Bribe?'' he echoed. ''I don't understand.''

''You give me work so that I leave you to conquer the coffee world?''

Now that was a leap. ''I'm wounded.''

''Sure you are. You're a clever man, Luke DeVries. I give you credit for that. Is there any woman you've failed to seduce?''

Seeing his plan backfire, he groaned. ''I think I've just run into one.''

Opening the iron gate, she said, "I'll be saying good-night now."

He stood there like a penniless kid with his nose pressed to a candy-store window. So close and yet so far away…

Without looking back, Helen unlocked the door and slipped inside. Luke waited until the interior lit up before he started walking toward his temporary home, probably the same distance as the SUV, only in the opposite direction. He could use the exercise.

But if he'd assumed Helen's presence was keeping him horny, he'd been wrong. She'd invaded his mind. All the way home, thoughts of her plagued him and he couldn't help but replay in his mind the intimate scenario at Hot Zone.

He was subletting an apartment in a warehouse conversion, and he took the old service elevator up to the fourth and top floor. Once in the apartment, he stripped, dropping clothing as he headed straight for the shower.

Helen Rhodes was still there in his mind, teasing him, making him want her.

Rather than turning the water on cold, he luxuriated in the pulsing hot stream while going over the brief sexual encounter. He imagined what it might have been like if Helen had invited him into her place.

If he didn't do something, he was going to go to bed with an erection. And even if he jerked off, he figured it was going to be a wet night. But at least that would give him temporary respite.

He soaped his cock and it filled his hand while Helen filled his mind.

She was all over him. Her lips. Her hands. She tore at his clothes. He helped her.

When she had him naked, his erection jutting out at her, she stood back and stared, her tongue darting out to wet her luscious mouth.

Oh, that mouth...that mouth was coming closer...but it wasn't aimed at his face. He held his breath waiting...watching. She went down to her knees...and surrounded him with the wet warmth of that lovely mouth.

"Oh, yes, darlin'," he muttered, tangling his fingers in her hair as he sank deeper inside.

She took in all of him—no mean feat—and he felt the soft palate at the back of her throat against his ultrasensitive tip. He groaned and fought the building pressure that screamed for release. Not yet, not this soon. He wanted more. He wanted to know what she would do to pleasure him.

Her mouth slipped along his length and when she got to his head did an unbelievable dance with her tongue and teeth. And then, with agonizing slowness, she sucked him, let him loose and slid home again.

Fighting it was no use. He couldn't hold out against her.

"I'm going to come," he said with a groan.

She slipped back and released him for an agonizing second. "That's good, isn't it?"

When she took him again, she cradled his balls and worked them gently one upon the other. Unable to hold back any longer, he let go of his grasp and felt his hot come pump into her mouth. She drank and drank and sucked him dry.

Then releasing his cock, she made greedy-sounding noises like she wanted more.

She ate her way up his stomach and along his abs, sucked at his nipples and then at his mouth.

Tasting himself, he drank deeply, plunging his tongue in her mouth the way he wanted to join his body to hers. But if he couldn't…

Shoving her over the edge of the chair, he spread her legs and then her lips, engorged and wet before he even touched her. He dipped the tip of his tongue along the creamy split and she arched to his mouth.

Even as he plunged his tongue deep inside her, his cock stirred. And when he surrounded her clit, sucked on it with a sex rhythm that had her writhing and moaning and begging for more, his cock grew erect again faster than he'd ever known it to.

Holding her hips, he pulled her closer, and teased her with his tip, an angry red to her seductive pink. She arched and lifted her legs, and with his encouragement hooked her ankles around his neck.

He slid into her slowly and controlled. Tweaked her nipples with increasing pressure until she slipped a hand between their bodies and cried out, ''Fuck me…hard!''

He drove into her and she echoed his force and speed with fingers that slid around his erection and against her own clit. She arched like a bow and made sexy guttural sounds that drove him faster and closer to losing his lode.

And when she cried out, "Now!" and shuddered, her sex squeezing him in a pulsing rhythm, he came.

Helen shuddered as the waves of her orgasm decreased in intensity, and she lay on her bed, naked, panting, wishing she wasn't alone. Wishing she hadn't had to indulge in fantasy. Wishing she hadn't had to gratify herself.

But Luke had opened Pandora's box, starting with that damn drink of his, and now Helen feared she wouldn't be able to lock it up again.

It had been far too long since she'd had satisfying intercourse. And even the pseudo-sex of the evening had been more satisfying than most of the lovemaking she'd experienced in her twenty-eight years.

She ached to feel a hard masculine body next to her. On her. In her.

Good heavens, how had she come to this?

She didn't want just any man...she ached for Luke DeVries!

"Don't be an idiot," she muttered, deciding to turn on her television to distract herself from thinking about him. Maybe she could catch the footage of the protest Nick had shot. That would set her priorities straight again.

Her bedroom being a lush cocoon of colored pillows, coverlets, curtains and upholstery of plum, rose and cream meant to satisfy her senses, the only electronics she'd allowed in here were a well-hidden surround-sound CD system and a tiny alarm clock disguised as an enameled treasure box next to her bed.

And then, of course, there was the vibrator safely tucked in her nightstand drawer. She hadn't even needed it tonight.

All she'd had to do was think about…

With a shriek, Helen slid out of bed. She would not think about him again tonight! Wrapping herself in a deep plum sheet, she shivered as the silk slid against her body. Her nipples sprang to life and the sensation quickly spread downward, planting itself between her thighs.

Quickly, she escaped the room of her fantasies, traipsing barefoot over her prized Oriental rug and down the stairs carpeted in a similar pattern. Her living room was as stark as the bedroom was plush.

Two lean-lined cream sofas, one on each side of the fireplace with its hand-carved wood mantel, faced each other. And on the wall opposite the fireplace, a cabinet of rich cherry wood hid her electronics. She opened the highly polished doors to reveal the television, VCR and DVD player. She might not have much in the way of furniture yet, but she couldn't do without her electronic toys.

The ten o'clock news had just started. She settled down on one of the couches, placing a velvet plum pillow behind her back. Stories about a shooting, political maneuvering between the mayor and governor and a potential teacher's strike when the schools reopened didn't interest her, but she tried concentrating on them anyway. Anything to get rid of the sexual buzz that still lingered.

When that didn't work, she muted the sound, breathed deeply and tried to meditate, but instead of seeing parklands and a sunrise over the lake, she saw dark eyes and a wicked smile that made her toes curl....

Suddenly realizing she was actually looking at Luke's face on television, Helen scooted up straighter and clicked the mute button again.

"Local businesspeople and neighbors marched against progress today, trying to stay the inevitable opening of Hot Zone, one of a chain of unique coffeehouses. Thirteenth in the chain, the Bucktown venue promised to be unlucky for owner Luke DeVries until he came face-to-face with the protest organizer and owner of Hot Zone's main competition."

The shot changed to one of her and Luke.

"Judging by her reaction to DeVries, it looks like the lady has a mind for compromise."

Catching her loopy smile as she looked up at Luke, a horrified Helen jumped up from the couch.

And when the camera cut back to the news anchors, they were grinning at each other knowingly. Before one of them could make the inevitable wisecrack, Helen used the remote to cut them off.

Feeling exposed—both figuratively and literally, since her sheet had fallen to the floor and she was standing buck naked in the middle of the living room—Helen turned her rage against Luke. He had to be responsible for turning a legitimate protest into a piece where no one would take her seriously.

A piece that hadn't even mentioned her name or the name of her café!

Somehow, Luke had turned her efforts to stop him into a joke and had gotten publicity for himself and Hot Zone all in one fell swoop.

And he thought she should *trust* him?

Helen whipped up the sheet from the floor and wrapped it around herself, all soft or sensual feelings driven out by her resentment.

He'd played her, the underhanded jerk.

Good thing they weren't dating.

4

"MAYBE YOU OUGHT to give the guy a break," Annie said when she and Nick joined Helen for their ritual morning coffee before Annie's Attic opened for the day. "Newspeople aren't actually known for having words put in their mouths."

"But Trevor Brandt is known for his wandering eye," Nick said.

"You're not intimating he and Luke—"

"No! He and Flash Gordon. That's DeVries's public relations director."

Wondering about the name, Helen asked, "How would you know that?"

"I got it from the horse's mouth. The horse's handler, anyway. The producer who said he'd run a clip. Apparently Ms. Flash got to Trevor."

Helen groaned. "Isn't that special! Wait until I get my hands on that Luke DeVries...."

"How can you be sure he even knew what Brandt would say ahead of time?"

Helen spoke through gritted teeth. "Because he's a control freak."

"Ooh, you've met your match," Nick said, ducking when she threw a packet of sugar at him.

Annie's eyebrows shot up over the top of her glasses. "Examples, please."

Though Helen felt her cheeks flame, she refused to let her friends bait her. "Isn't it time you opened up shop?"

"Gloria will do it." Gloria Delgado was Annie's capable assistant manager. "So what aren't you telling us?"

"Yeah, spill," Nick said, suddenly bright-eyed and bushy-tailed, undoubtedly at the prospect of getting something juicy on her.

"One of these days, I'll spill something on you, all right."

"More threats," Nick grumbled and met Annie's gaze. "It must be something really good."

"Don't worry," Annie said in a pseudo-whisper, "*I'll* spill when she tells me."

Gaping at them both, Helen plunged to her feet. "I have real customers to wait on!"

Nick looked around at the mostly empty café. Rush hour had come and gone and they were in the long lull before lunch. "Yeah, I can see that."

When the door opened, Helen sighed with relief and almost bolted to her spot at the register.

She would work the café alone for the next couple of hours. A college kid helped with the morning rush, then her assistant manager Kate reported for work before lunch and stayed until closing. Other part-timers worked the lunch and evening rush as necessary.

But for the next hour or so, she was it, and so when

the door opened again and in walked Luke DeVries, she felt trapped.

"Good morning, can I help you?" she asked, her voice purposely cool.

"You saw the newscast. A Breve, please."

"Certainly. You must have gotten a good laugh last night. Regular size or large?"

"Not at all. I had very different emotions, actually. Large."

"And then this morning you must have congratulated your PR person—and what kind of name is Flash Gordon anyway? Three dollars."

"Actually, I stopped by to apologize," he said, sliding the money to her.

"You what?"

"I have to admit I was relieved not to get negative publicity right before the opening, but the last thing I wanted was for you to feel foolish."

Helen swallowed hard. He was apologizing. He seemed sincere. Could she believe him?

Could she *trust* him?

"So you didn't know anything about it?"

"Flash told me she handled it. She just didn't tell me how. I didn't ask."

"A crime of omission rather than commission." But her accusation held less hostility than was warranted.

"I really am sorry. Will you forgive me? Give me another chance?"

"A chance at what?"

Luke looked around and Helen's gaze followed his.

Only Tilda, the homeless woman, lingered at a table by the windows.

"Can we sit and talk for a moment?" he asked.

Helen couldn't help herself. Her anger and resentment had faded in the face of his apology.

"For a moment," she agreed, coming around the counter and following him to a table. She sat across from him.

He glanced around him. "This place is nice. Comfortable. Appealing. Totally unlike mine."

"Now you're saying that Hot Zone isn't nice?" Helen couldn't keep the disbelief from her tone.

"I'm saying it's seductive while yours is a great place to...well, work or simply pass the time. They each inspire different wants."

She couldn't argue with that. "Is that why you're here? To tell me again that you're no threat to me...uh, to my business."

"I'm not. Not to the café." He put on a slow grin. "Now *you're* a different matter."

Pulse accelerating, she asked, "What do you want, Luke?"

"You. On a date. On a *first* date," he emphasized.

"Why?"

"Last night."

"What about it?"

"I couldn't get you out of my mind."

"Back at you." One way or another, he'd dominated her whole evening. "Though I would say our thoughts were quite different."

Not exactly a lie. Once she'd seen the newscast,

she'd imagined different ways of torturing him, none of which involved sex. If only she had remembered her original resolve—to get him to spill, as Nick would put it—she would feel a whole lot better.

Wouldn't she?

Purposely filing the sexual satisfaction he'd given her to the back of her mind, she decided she deserved another try at finding out what his real intentions were—as a businessman.

"So this will be an official date."

Helen was thankful she hadn't explained her date rule in detail. Let him think what he wanted. Let him think he'd get her into bed. But if she so much as thought about letting him get to the first stage with her, she should have her head examined.

"Unless we end up talking business," Luke amended. "Then we have to start the count over."

Hmm, now how was she going to manage to get information out of him without actually talking business? And why should she care about her date rule, anyway, why should she care that after three dates she'd have to cut him off?

"Fair enough." Whatever he wanted to hear. If she concentrated on her purpose, all she needed was this one shot anyway. "And you'll forget about last night?"

His lips stretched into a grin. "I will if you will."

Great. Her body was already responding.

But she kept a bland expression plastered to her face when she said, "And we're not going to have sex."

"No sex?" came a quavering voice. "Helen, honey, what are you thinking?" The old homeless woman had wandered up to them and was standing there, shaking her head.

"Tilda!"

"You pass up sex with this good-looking fella, *you're* the one who's crazy," Tilda muttered as she continued on her way to the rest room.

Luke laughed outright, making Helen flush.

Helen looked at Luke to see his reaction. He was enjoying this. She narrowed her gaze at him.

"What? I didn't say anything."

"No, you're just smirking."

"Define smirk."

"It's that know-it-all expression you're wearing."

"And that would be wrong because...?"

Because she didn't want him to have the advantage.

Luckily, a customer came in just then, giving her a reprieve.

"I need to get this."

Helen whipped out of her seat and rushed to the counter, giving the customer her undivided attention. And when she looked back a few minutes later, all that was left at the table was Luke's discarded cup.

"Morning," Kate called as she sailed through the door.

"You're early."

"Ten minutes. No biggie."

Surprised, Helen checked her watch. Sure enough, it was later than she'd thought. Time flew when you were being aggravated.

As Kate rounded the counter, Luke came out of the rest room.

"There you are," she muttered.

"Afraid I'd left without saying goodbye?"

"Does your sense of importance know any bounds?"

"When warranted, of course."

Meaning he figured he had her and didn't have to work at it, a sentiment that raised her ire. If Helen hated anything, it was being taken for granted.

A dark-haired young woman entered, her gaze immediately fixing on Luke. "Hey, boss, there you are."

"Alexis. Problem?"

"Flash wants you. Photo op."

"Where?"

"Hot Zone."

Helen listened to their shorthand-style conversation in amazement, suspecting that it came with their knowing one another very well.

Luke looked to Helen. "This is my assistant, Alexis Stark. She set up last night for us."

"Great dinner," Helen jumped in lest Luke hint at anything more. "Thanks."

"Uh-huh. Whatever the boss wants, he gets."

A statement that Helen feared was too true.

"Duty calls," he said, heading for the door.

"Don't let me get in the way of a promo opportunity."

"I know you don't mean that. We'll talk later," he promised.

"Hey, how's the coffee here?" Alexis asked him.

"First rate." He gave Helen a thumbs-up as he opened the door.

And Helen noted the way the young woman looked longingly after her boss—she was clearly smitten with him.

"I'll catch up, Luke," Alexis said. "I need a caffeine fix."

"What can I get you?" Kate asked, setting herself up at the register.

Alexis said, "A Breve."

The same thing Luke had ordered, Helen noted. Choosing to bury herself in work until the lunch hour traffic started, she sat at a computer and brought up the Web page she'd been working on earlier.

"Hmm, out of cream up here," she heard Kate say. "Hang on. I'll get another carton from the back."

Having trouble concentrating, Helen imagined Luke's assistant was wandering around, checking over the café, sneaking looks at her. So, had Luke's employee set up other such dinner dates for him? she wondered. That must make her feel terrible, considering how she obviously felt.

But "whatever the boss wants," she'd said.

Helen forced her mind to focus on the work, looking up only for a moment when the outer door opened and a couple of teenage girls entered. Then she began playing with fonts for the Muscle Beach Juice Bar menu.

"I'll be right with you," she heard Kate say.

Helen glanced back and saw a redhead at the

counter with Alexis and realized she'd been so engrossed for a while that she hadn't heard the second woman come in. But this was hardly a woman who could be missed with her flaming-red hair, sleek dress and stiletto heels.

Towering over Alexis, she was saying something to Luke's assistant in low tones. Something that was making Alexis decidedly unhappy. A co-worker? From the looks of her, this woman could be in promotions, and Helen wondered if this was the infamous Flash Gordon, who she had to thank for her embarrassment the night before.

But before she could get up to find out for certain, Alexis grabbed her coffee and stormed past the redhead and out the door, brushing past a couple of regulars—Laura and her little girl, Jenny—who were in the process of entering. Seeming irritated also, the redhead swept out of the place as if she couldn't leave fast enough.

Hmm, so what had that intense conversation been about? Helen wondered.

Though she tried to get back to work on the Muscle Beach Web site, it was no use. Every time she looked at a male body beautiful, she thought of Luke. Besides, business was picking up.

Twenty minutes later she and Kate and one of the part-timers were inundated with customers.

Suddenly, the sound of a slammed door cut over customer chatter as did Laura's raised voice. "Come on, honey, we're getting out of here now!" She was dragging her daughter from the rest room toward the front door.

''Is something wrong?'' Helen asked.

''Yes, something is definitely wrong and I won't be coming back! I won't subject my child to druggies.''

''I don't understand. What happened?''

''Look in your rest room!'' she said, dragging her daughter Jenny out the door.

Helen rushed back to the women's rest room but saw nothing. No needles. No bags. No pills. She sniffed the air, but all she smelled was the deodorizer tablet discreetly attached to the wall.

Then she spotted them—three white lines of powder laid out on the small table between the sink and toilet. A sick feeling knotting her stomach, Helen thought to flush what must be cocaine. But that would be getting rid of evidence. Not knowing what to do, she fetched a resealable bag from the kitchen and scooped the powder into it. Then after stuffing the bag into her pocket, she went back into the café.

''So what's going on?'' Kate asked.

Helen shrugged, said, ''Later,'' and got back to the customers.

Was it her imagination, or were there fewer than there ought to be for this time of the afternoon? Had Laura's announcement driven some away?

Sam was working at his homework and Tilda was working on a fresh cup. The teenage girls were playing Internet games and a businessman was reading the stock reports online. But usually all the computers were in use this time of day.

Praying this was a fluke, she concentrated on the orders until the lunch rush was past.

"So are you going to give or what?" Kate asked then, forcing Helen to face the problem whether or not she wanted to.

"There's nothing to give." Not until she had a plan, anyway. "Hold down the fort, will you?"

"Yeah, sure."

Helen left and rounded the corner. She looked into Annie's Attic, but her friend was busy with a customer. So she went on to the next doorway and took the stairs up to Nick's Knack. She knew he would be there, busy editing footage for Club Undercover down the street.

"What's up?" he asked, the moment she opened the door and poked her head in.

"I have a problem and need your opinion."

She entered Nick's combination studio and editing area with its racks of equipment. The trundle bed still sat in one corner, but she knew he rarely spent the night here anymore. Why should he when he could spend it with Isabel at her place? And when Isabel's sister Louise went off to college in a few weeks, he would officially move in with his ladylove.

Helen set the plastic bag on his console and waited for him to finish an edit.

"What is it?" Nick asked as he picked up the bag.

"One of my customers said something about druggies using the rest room. I found this laid out in lines and now I don't know what to do with it.''

He already had the bag open and his nose was half inside. Pulling back, he sneezed.

''Someone left talcum powder laid out in lines?''

''Powder?''

''Smell it.''

Helen lifted the bag to her nose. The scent was distinctive. ''You're right. I don't get it.''

Nick shrugged. ''Either someone was fooled into buying talcum powder rather than cocaine...or someone has a sick sense of humor.''

''That's sick, all right!'' she said, chucking the bag into a trash container.

Rather than being angry, she was simply relieved. ''I'll have to tell Laura she was mistaken...if she ever comes back, that is.''

''Any idea of who might think this was funny? It seems like something a kid would do.''

Helen shrugged. ''It's kind of a blur. We were really busy at the time. It could have been anyone. Hmm, not too long before it happened, a couple of teenaged girls came in.''

Relieved or not, Helen wanted to pin back their ears and scare them within an inch of their lives for being so thoughtless. But at least she could breathe again.

''That *could* explain it,'' Nick agreed.

''You have another theory.''

''Nah.''

But she knew he did. ''What?''

"It's kind of odd how nothing like this ever happened before..."

"Before what?"

"Never mind."

Before Hot Zone was set to open?

Luke had been in the men's rest room, right next to the women's, she remembered.

"Luke wouldn't do something like this," she said, wondering why she was so quick to defend him.

"No, of course not."

"Anyway, thanks," she said, leaning over and kissing his cheek.

Nick couldn't hide his surprise. Helen knew it was because, while they would do anything for each other, they rarely let their affection show. Normally, Nick tried to verbally torture her and she enjoyed giving as good as she got.

"Getting soft?" he asked.

"Ooh, I lost my head. It won't happen again, I promise. Um, I'd better get back to the coffee brigade."

"Later," Nick said, turning back to his equipment.

About to leave, Helen caught a glimpse of the piece he was working on. He'd gotten footage of Isabel and her sister. They looked so happy. And when a closeup of Isabel appeared on the screen, she was absolutely radiant as she smiled into the camera. Rather, smiled at Nick.

Helen recognized the look—Annie wore it, as well, whenever she was around Nate.

As she closed the door behind her, Helen wondered

if she would ever have that in common with her best friends—knowing what it felt like to be unashamedly in love.

''HAVE YOU GOTTEN much resistance from the communities where you've opened venues in the past?'' Sam Bobek asked.

The baby-faced reporter from the local newspaper was grilling Luke as Flash sailed in the door and spotted them. He waved his public relations director over to the hot-tub area where the tour Luke had been giving the reporter had stalled. He'd been prepared for a photo opportunity, not the third degree. But even before the photographer had finished documenting the layout, the reporter had started in on him.

''It's understandable that an innovative business would raise a few eyebrows,'' Luke admitted.

He didn't want to get into a mud-throwing contest, not when Helen was the one who'd organized the protestors. He wanted to keep his relationship with her smooth.

But Bobek seemed determined to spice up his story with conflict when he said, ''Hot Zone has done more than raise eyebrows—''

''For a handful of people who will be happy that we're here once we're in operation,'' Flash said, smoothing things over in her inimitable fashion. ''I have statistics on the upsurge in traffic for many local businesses in neighborhoods where we've opened in the past. A healthy economic growth is inevitable, considering we'll be bringing new people into the area. If you would care to take a look..."

"Bring it on."

"Wonderful, the office is upstairs. Can you wait for me in the foyer? I'll be with you in a minute."

The reporter signaled his photographer and they both headed for the entrance.

"You saved the day," Luke said.

"Just making myself indispensable," she said, spinning on her heel and following the two men.

And she'd been doing a good job of it, Luke thought. Hot Zone might be his vision, but he hadn't gotten this far on his own.

Myriad people had made significant contributions to the legend of his foresight, including several talented architects and designers. But he had to give equal credit to the woman who'd not only started the buzz about Hot Zone, but had kept it going and growing.

And Flash's reputation as a primo publicist had grown with the business, so much so that he wondered what kept her working for him. Not that he didn't reward her well for her services. But why pick up and move around so much when she could have her choice of jobs—and stability, as well? He'd asked her once and she'd claimed that *he* was the reason. That his vision challenged her.

He had real loyalty in Flash Gordan.

And in Alexis Stark, Luke thought, adding his assistant to the successful mix when he spotted her heading toward him. He tended to overlook the dependable young woman's contribution at times, maybe because she didn't have a specific skill. But she'd also been with him from the beginning and took care of all the odd jobs, from seeing that he got to his business appointments on time to making his personal arrangements—whatever needed to be done—usually with good cheer.

Only she wasn't looking so cheerful this afternoon, he noted. "What's up?"

"I was going to ask you the same. Is there anything I need to do for you this afternoon? Set up another tête-à-tête with Ms. Rhodes?"

"I think I can take care of things on that end myself."

Silent for a moment, Alexis asked, "So you *are* seeing her again?"

"Tonight."

"Oh...well...if you don't need me, mind if I cut out early?"

"No. Go." Noticing she appeared a bit pale, he asked, "Is everything all right?"

Alexis shrugged and backed off.

"Want to talk about it?"

"I don't think it would do any good," she said. "See you in the morning, okay?"

"Fine."

She was probably just tired, Luke thought, wondering if he was working her too hard.

But before he could think it through, the massage chairs caught his eye and his mind went on a different trajectory altogether.

Helen Rhodes. He hadn't been prepared for her. Hadn't been prepared for the depth of his attraction. He'd always enjoyed women, but this one topped them all.

She invaded his sleep. Invaded his thoughts when he should have been concentrating on all the last-minute details that awaited his attention.

Even now, he could see her golden blond curls in artful disarray. He could stare out into space and suddenly space turned into the emerald depths of eyes punctuated by a tiny mole at one corner. And if he let himself go, he could feel her body pressed tightly against his own.

He found it difficult to concentrate with a near-continual hard-on for the woman.

A problem he hoped would be resolved that very evening.

5

''REMEMBER, ANY REFERENCE to business makes this a nondate, which would mean the count starts over,'' Luke reminded Helen as a second round of margaritas arrived.

They were having drinks at the restaurant atop the North Avenue Beach facility, a building that resembled an ocean liner, except with changing rooms and bike rentals and a newspaper stand on the ground floor. The place itself wasn't fancy, but, ah, the surroundings. Out on the beach below, a few volleyball games were still in progress despite the fading light. Breakers rolled in over the sand and the city skyline twinkled as the sun set, leaving the darkening sky streaked with pink and orange.

Her enjoyment of the romantic setting superseded her worry over the drug prank—simply not Luke's style, Helen convinced herself. Despite her determination to protect her business interests, she was enjoying herself.

''So if we can't talk business, what *do* we talk about?'' Helen asked.

''The view?''

''Gorgeous.''

"Weather?"

"Pleasant, considering it's August."

Indeed, a lake breeze swept over them, swirling the silk of her sari skirt around her legs, bringing the temperature down to a comfortable level.

"The drinks?"

"Tasty."

"You're just itching to do it, aren't you?" he asked.

"Do what?"

"Make this a nondate."

Bristling at the challenge in his voice, Helen demurred, "Of course not." Though this was supposed to be anything but a date for her, she felt herself softening toward him, yearning for something she shouldn't want. The margaritas must be addling her brain. Perhaps she'd better stop drinking. "I was simply trying to set the ground rules." She took just one more salty, sweet-sour slurp and put the glass down on the table.

"I thought you already did that with your 'three strikes and he's out' dating philosophy. Or is there more to them? Maybe you can illuminate."

No way was she about to explain further. She wasn't about to get to any stage with him tonight. Information, that was what she wanted.

Wasn't it?

Simply looking at Luke sitting back all relaxed, top two buttons of his shirt undone, wind ruffling his spiked hair, Helen wished things were different. She wished he was just some guy she'd met at a party or at the grocery store. A guy who had no vested interests in anything that could be considered competition.

"How about *you* doing the illuminating?" she suggested, trying to keep herself on track. "Where are you from originally?"

"Florida, Wyoming, Maryland, California, Louisiana, New Mexico, Texas, Mississippi, New Jersey, Alaska, South Carolina, Alabama. Pick one."

"Wow. I don't think I've ever known anyone who moved around that much."

"My dad was career military. Air force."

"That had to be hard on you. I remember hating moving, even though it was to nicer places both times, but at least I've lived right here in Chicago all my life."

Luke shrugged. "You're just lucky your father had steady work in one city."

"Not my father...my mom."

"Oh, sorry. Divorce can be hard on a kid, as well." He reached out and covered her hand with his, prompting a shock that went straight up her arm.

"Uh-huh," she murmured evasively, unwilling to correct him. Heat slid from her shoulder to her neck and she squirmed in her seat a bit. Not because her father had never seen fit to marry her mom, but because Luke was so tempting.

She pulled her hand free, grabbed her drink and took a long sip.

"Actually, my mom died when I was a kid," Luke said.

Swallowing hard, she felt a wave of sympathy for

him. Or perhaps empathy, knowing what it was like to have only one parent in her life. "So your dad never gave you a stepmother?"

"He did. Three, actually. He would get lonely and marry too quickly, without giving the woman a true picture of what life in the air force was going to be like. Or maybe he did and they didn't believe him. Who knows? But none of those marriages lasted more than a few years. But he's retired now and he met an army widow who can keep him in line."

How ironic. She had a mother who'd never married and he had a father who'd married too often.

Somehow, that made her feel more connected to Luke, a fact that should have been more disturbing than it was. She wasn't supposed to be connecting, she was supposed to be figuring out how to survive in shark-infested waters.

But if Luke was a shark, she had to admit he was a very subtle, very attractive one.

"Siblings?" she asked.

"A half sister twenty years younger. I hardly know Peggy. I've only seen her a few times. Her mother remarried and had two more kids, so she doesn't need me."

Thinking of her own half siblings, Helen said, "You don't know that. Have you tried having a relationship with her?"

"Relationships aren't my strong suit."

And no wonder. His own life had lacked the stability a kid needed, the stability her mom had been careful to give her. No doubt every time he'd made friends he'd had to leave them behind to go on to the next air force base. Maybe that's why he'd picked a business where he didn't have to stay in one place, Helen thought. Apparently he was carrying on the tradition of not getting too close to anyone for long.

Well, that fit in with her plans perfectly.

Whoa...wait a minute. Plans? Was she drunk? She must be, because the idea of covering the three bases over three dates with Luke DeVries was suddenly looking very, very appealing.

Why not? What would it hurt? a little voice demanded. *You want to...you know you do.*

"So does your mother still live in Chicago?" Luke asked, jerking her out of her thoughts.

"She does. Right over there as a matter of fact." Helen pointed to a high-rise apartment complex towering over Lake Shore Drive.

He whistled. "Fancy location."

"A long way from the south-side neighborhood where she grew up," Helen agreed. "Mom only has a small one bedroom, but she adores her lake view and loves living downtown. No need for a car. She can walk to work. She's the senior buyer at one of our upscale department stores."

"No doubt where you get your fashion sense."

Helen laughed. "Hardly. Although I do use her discount every once in a while, we have *very* different tastes in clothing. She's a dynamite lady, though. Worked her way up from the clerk's job she had when I was a kid."

Luke's expression was odd, as if he were reassessing her. Then he asked, "Siblings?"

And Helen sobered. "Half brother and sister. My father's children. They want nothing to do with me. And, yes, I'm sure of that. They don't even recognize my existence."

Luke's forehead furrowed. "Now that has to be rough."

"I don't even think about it anymore," she lied, polishing off that second margarita, after all.

"I don't believe that. I suspect it bothers you tremendously."

"You're right," she said. "Okay, so you're right. My own father never wanted me, so why should they?"

Luke didn't so much as hesitate before saying, "Because you're a smart, hardworking, very engaging woman that anyone should be proud to claim."

Helen put it to her tequila-induced state, but something inside her softened and she suddenly wanted to get closer to Luke. Wanted this to be a real date.

And who would be more perfect to date than a man who wouldn't stay around long enough to exceed her rules?

But what if those rumors about his sinking other businesses are true? another voice asked. *What if he did use shady tactics to put his competition out of business?*

Now that she knew him personally, Helen didn't want to believe it of Luke.

Besides, it simply didn't make sense. His business

was so high concept that it would succeed or die on its own merit, no matter the competition, because nothing could touch it. Hoping that Kate had been right—that all businesses had problems, and who knew how much of what she'd heard or even read had been based on fact?—Helen decided to go for it.

HAND IN HAND, they strolled down the walkway edging the beach. The night was lush, the lake enticing with its wash of breakers kissing the sand, the walkway a danger to anyone not on a bike or roller blades, even at this late hour.

"Let's take off our shoes and cut across the sand before one of us is wearing a bike," Luke suggested, also wanting to get Helen off to himself.

"All right."

She stepped off the walkway and out of her sandals in a second. He took a bit longer and had to catch up to her. Finding her hand, he threaded his fingers through hers.

"You're unexpectedly agreeable," he noted.

"It's the tequila."

"Uh-uh. You ate enough for two people. You're so stone-cold sober, I'd bet anything you could walk a straight line."

Rather than make another excuse, she merely smiled at him in answer, and he felt his chest and gut tighten.

They walked in silence, kicking up the cool, loose sand, Luke returning to the conversation about families and wondering how any man could turn his back on a child that he'd sired. Wondering how siblings could turn their backs on a sister. Though she'd tried to hide it, he'd heard hurt ripe in Helen's voice. Right then, he'd decided to call his kid sister the next morning. Though Peggy probably was too young to know it now, she needed him. And he needed her. And he hadn't even realized it before.

He really *was* lousy at relationships.

Helen stopped suddenly and lifted her head to the breeze. Her curls fluttered back from her face, as did the split skirt, the silken panels dancing behind her, revealing her long, luscious legs to the swirling sands. Luke stepped away to take a better look. Moonlight silvered her from head to toe, and he was reminded of a goddess.

Music played from a nearby boom box, its owners spread on a blanket necking hot and heavy. There was something about that Latin rhythm, Luke thought, noticing Helen's hips were swaying to the music. Grasping her wrist lightly, he swung Helen around and into his arms, making her drop her sandals.

"What?" she gasped.

Dropping his sandals next to hers, he murmured, "Let's dance." He pulled her closer and rotated his hips against hers in a slow, sensual rumba.

No sex, she'd said earlier when he'd asked her out.

Surely she hadn't been serious, not after that spectacular orgasm he'd given her the night before. Maybe she simply meant she didn't want to go any further. Well, that was all right with him. For the moment.

They might as well be having sex right now, he thought, for their moving together across the sand was as erotic as any lovemaking. His erection grew at dizzying proportions, making his head grow light. All he could think about was burying himself in this woman, feeling her legs wrap around his back and grip him as he rode her to climax.

And then the music died, replaced by a rapid-fire commercial in Spanish, and the mood was broken. Helen stepped back out of his arms, her moonlit face wreathed in a dreamy expression, making Luke want to take her right there.

"Let's get our feet wet," she said, picking up her sandals and heading straight for the water.

Luke followed at a more deliberate pace.

Helen was holding her skirts up now, bunching them above her knees as she splashed into the shallows and shrieked. "Brr, it's cold!"

"I could use that cold water on more than my feet," he muttered. "Too bad I didn't bring a suit."

"You could skinny-dip."

"I will if you will."

"And get arrested for indecent exposure? Not my style."

But once in his mind, the image wouldn't fade. The goddess Helen standing nude in the surf, breakers crashing around her thighs, the nipples of her full heavy breasts tight from the cold. He imagined drawing her deeper into the lake, where he could warm her with his own body....

Instead, he splashed alongside the woman and let

her take the lead back in the direction of the beach house and parking lot. They stopped on the walkway to dust sand off their feet and put on their sandals.

"Your place or mine?" Luke asked.

"I think my place is safer."

"Why is that?"

"Yours is too seductive."

"Just the effect I was going for."

"Then you were very successful," Helen agreed, furtively glancing around, "but remember what I said this morning."

Realizing she was speaking in code because of the people still wandering along the beach, Luke smirked. "You said a lot of things this morning."

She gave him an arch look. "I'm sure you remember this *particular* thing."

"Oh, I remember every word you said, darlin'." No sex? Hah! "But after last night, I don't understand why."

"Last night was an aberration." She actually sounded appalled at herself.

"Are you saying you've never done those things?"

"Of course I have! Just not so soon. I don't even know you. Um, about my three-date rule…"

"You're going to suspend it?" he asked hopefully.

"I was going to explain it."

"I thought it was pretty simple."

"It is. First date, kissing…second date, touching…"

Then it hit him. And third date, the big payoff. That meant she never slept with a man more than once, something he couldn't fathom, because having her once surely wouldn't be enough.

"First date," he repeated softly. "Kissing? That's as far as you go on a first date?"

"It works for me."

"All right, then." Luke would find a way to make kissing work for him, too. "Let's get going."

Helen rose, dusted off her hands and turned to go to the car, but Luke caught her by the wrist and twirled her back around to face him. Before she could voice the question he noted in her eyes, he brushed his lips over hers. Her quick intake of breath pleased him, and he was about to kiss her again, when someone shouted, "Hey, get outta the way!"

He drew her from the path of the cyclist and against him with only inches to spare.

"Slow down!"

In response, the cyclist gave him the finger.

"Nice," Helen murmured.

Luke noticed she didn't try to pull away. Her breath deepened and her pulse quickened—he could feel it where he held her. Wanting in the worst way to give her a first date like she'd never before experienced, he let go of her and took her hand.

"C'mon."

They headed for the parking lot.

Mere minutes later, they stopped at the SUV. Luke opened the door for Helen, then kissed her again. He made this one long and sweet and hoped to hell her knees were turning to jelly. He had to hold on to the frame of the vehicle to steady himself. Unless he figured an angle here, he was going to have another wet night.

When he pulled away, her eyes were wide on him and she was swallowing hard. Good signs, Luke thought, helping her inside. He clung to her hand for a moment and kissed her palm. Her fingers curled reflexively.

Once out of the lot and heading for home, Luke said, "Define kiss."

"I don't think you need any help in that direction. You know, that thing you do with your mouth."

"So that's it?" He lifted her hand toward his face. "I can only use my lips?" He kissed the inside of her wrist and heard the subtle shift in her breathing. "I want to get my parameters straight here."

"Well...lips and associated parts."

"Okay, lips, teeth and tongue." He sucked on a fingertip, then bit it lightly. "No hands?"

"Nowhere intimate."

"And that's it? That's the whole enchilada?"

"I told you my dating rules were simple." Helen laughed. "I keep getting drawn into the strangest conversations with you. How is that?"

"You like me. And you want to throw away your rules, and you're hoping I'll talk you out of them. Am I right or am I right?"

Helen merely laughed again, but Luke didn't miss the edge that told him he was square on target.

WHERE THE HELL WERE THEY? Not at Hot Zone—she'd already checked. That's why she was waiting here, practically in Helen's front yard.

Seeing another vehicle coming down the street, she drew herself into the neighboring bushes. An SUV…two people in the front seat…bingo!

Luke parked down the block, helped Helen out and they took their time walking back. Every so often, he would stop and kiss the bitch!

When would he kiss *her* like that? she wondered.

He will, a little voice whispered. *It won't be long now. You'll show him you're the better woman…the right partner for him.*

But, in the meantime, she would have to suffer another of his fast females.

They were on the porch now, kissing again. And then Helen was getting her keys and opening her front door. She turned back to Luke and started to say something, but he kissed her again and pushed her back through the doorway.

The door slammed shut behind them.

Her stomach knotted.

She didn't want to know, so why had she come here? Just to torture herself? But he'd never before dated his chief competitor….

She whipped away from the bushes and hurried down the street. She had more important things to do. Plans to make. Businesses to destroy.

Helen's business.

This time she would enjoy it as she never had before.

This time it would be personal.

LUKE TRAILED KISSES down the length of her neck and dangerously near her breasts. Her nipples hardened and he was close enough that he must see them stabbing at him through the thin silk of her midriff top.

"W-what are you doing?" she gasped, letting her weight fall against the back of the couch.

"Kissing you."

"You missed. My mouth is a bit higher."

"Uh-uh. I'm simply following the rules you made. You didn't say anything about *where* I could kiss you."

His tongue dipped down into her cleavage. Her whole body tightened in anticipation of something that was not going to happen. Her fingers tightened on the couch back.

"You're being too literal!"

"I'm sticking to the spirit of the rule," Luke murmured as he continued to work his lips down her torso. When he reached the hem of the midriff top, he nudged it out of the way.

She thought to protest.

He kissed the soft flesh of her belly.

She opened her mouth to tell him to stop.

His tongue found her navel.

Nothing came out of her mouth but a soft moan.

He scraped his teeth on the flesh along the low rise of her skirt. Sensation bolted downward and suddenly Helen's legs felt like rubber. She was grateful for the solid furniture behind her.

Closing her eyes, she thought to allow herself to be swept away just for a tiny moment. She felt Luke's hands stroke her ankles, then work their way up the sides of her calves.

Reveling in the pleasure he was giving her, she realized he was kissing his way downward through the silks of her skirts. She was so hot, she could hardly stand it.

"Uh, Luke?"

"Hmm?"

He made the sound with his mouth right over her pubic bone and it vibrated straight down to her center. His hands were on her thighs now, smoothing the flesh as he moved his fingers between and parted them.

She opened her eyes to see him kneeling before her and she knew what he was about to do. She should protest, tell him he was taking his creativity too far.

Instead, she gripped the couch harder, spread her legs wider and said, "Yes, yes, kiss me there."

He pushed her skirts out of his way and kissed her as she'd asked, his lips brushing her center, his teeth moving her thong to the side, his tongue slipping into the creamy folds now revealed to him.

Unable to help herself, she encouraged him by rocking against his mouth. His hands cupped her tush, tilting and opening her more fully. Then his mouth covered her and drank her in like a thirsty man who'd found an oasis in the middle of a desert.

Her kissed flesh swelled and pulsed and yearned for something just out of reach.

And just when she thought she couldn't stand it

another second, his mouth was moving again, upward, skimming her belly and the valley between her breasts. His lips followed the length of her throat, tested the line of her jaw, then settled over her mouth.

Tasting herself on him, she was ready for anything, but he broke the kiss and stepped back.

"Good night," he whispered.

Dazed, she thought she heard wrong. "What?"

He brushed his lips over hers once more. "I said...good night."

He was going to leave? Now? Her body protested. She was speechless.

He started to pull away.

"Wait!"

It was Luke's turn to be speechless. He stared at her, eyebrows arched in silent question.

Helen stewed, not wanting to seem too easy, not wanting to flagrantly break her own rule.

Not wanting him to leave...not wanting this incredible experience to end...not yet.

"Basically, you were doing all the kissing," she pointed out.

His lips curled into a smile that shot straight through her. "What do you suggest?"

"A little reciprocation is in order."

"Fair is fair," he agreed.

She stepped closer and his smile faded. Tension wired from him to her as their mouths met in a deep, hungry, soul-searing kiss. She tangled her fingers in his hair and held on for the ride.

When they broke away, panting, foreheads pressed

together, Helen nipped at his lower lip. Luke grunted but didn't move away, so she scraped her teeth along his jaw and aimed for his ear. She tested the lobe with her teeth, then lined the shell with her tongue.

Luke pulled her hips closer so that she could feel the length and strength of his erection against her belly. She kissed the side of his neck, then bit the soft flesh where it met his shoulder. His erection stirred and she felt wet warmth pool between her thighs.

She wanted him in her, drenched and slick with her juices. She could see it in her mind's eye as she kissed the base of his throat and worked her way down his body, as he had hers. Fishing out the tab with her tongue, she used her teeth to unzip his pants, her hands to undo the hook. It took every fiber of strength not to touch him as she longed to do.

The thin silky briefs couldn't hide his reaction to her. She ran her lips along the bulge and felt him stir. Wanting to give as good as she'd gotten, she worked him with lips, teeth and tongue as he'd done her until she was certain he was close to coming.

Then she rose, sensuously drawing her body along his, kissed him on the mouth and murmured, "Good night." She hooked his trousers back together.

"That's it?" he croaked.

"Fair is fair," she said, echoing him.

Luke nodded and zipped up his pants as he backed toward the door. His voice was tight as he said, "See you in your dreams, darlin'."

"You, too." She kissed him again, lightly this time, and opened the door.

He brushed his lips over hers one last time before walking out into the night.

Helen closed the door behind Luke and leaned back against it, thinking, orgasm or no orgasm, that was some of the best sex she'd ever experienced in her life.

6

"WAIT A MINUTE, wasn't last night date number *two?*" Annie asked after Helen told her all about her evening with Luke.

Well, not *all* about it, just the dinner and beach part.

"That's the way I would have called it, but Luke didn't exactly agree. Since we talked business that first time, he said it didn't count as a date."

Having left his computer station where he'd been surfing the net, Nick twirled a chair around backward and sat. "Since when does the guy get to screw around with your rules?" He gaped at her. "Uh-oh, you like Luke DeVries."

"Of course I like him or I wouldn't go out with him in the first place."

"No, not that kind of like. I mean *like* with a big *L* that also stands for *lusting* after the guy...getting *lucky*...falling in *love*..."

"He has his, um...charms...but don't get ahead of yourself," Helen said, hoping that Nick would drop it.

Not a chance.

His expression smug, he locked gazes with Annie.

"Well, what do you know about that? Our Helen has finally taken the tumble. About time, wouldn't you say?"

"No one's tumbling here!"

But Annie rode right over her objection. "Maybe we should throw a rule-burning party in Luke's honor."

Sorry that she hadn't immediately changed the subject when Annie had asked for details, Helen protested, "I wouldn't go that far."

"How far *would* you go?" the other woman asked.

"How far *did* you go last night?" Nick wanted to know, looking something like a vulture focusing on a potentially tasty meal.

Helen felt heat creep up her neck and into her cheeks. "I follow my own rules, thank you very much." She pretended interest in the dregs in her coffee cup.

"If you did follow your own rules, then last night should have been the second date," Annie insisted.

"Well, it just wasn't, but don't read something into it that's not there."

Nick shifted his chair closer and lowered his voice as if he didn't want to be heard by the handful of customers spread around the café. "So you didn't do anything more than kiss the guy good-night?"

Why had she ever explained her damn rules to Nick? Helen wondered. "Um, pretty much." She never could lie to her friends.

"You 'pretty much' kissed him?"

"That's my story and I'm sticking to it." Before

they could hound her for more intimate details, Helen said, ''Don't either of you have work to do?''

Annie checked her watch and practically flew to her feet. ''Yikes! Gloria's coming in late today.''

''Wait a minute,'' Nick said. ''I'm previewing my new video footage at Club Undercover Friday night. I thought maybe we could all go together.''

''Sure,'' Annie said.

Helen added, ''Sounds like a plan.''

Annie kissed Helen's cheek. ''I'll have my fingers crossed for you where Luke is concerned.''

''Not necessary...''

But Annie was already gone. And Nick was standing there, grinning at her. He was enjoying her discomfort, that was for certain. She could practically hear his strategies to get to her rattling around in his head.

''Don't.''

He simply grinned harder.

''Helen,'' Kate called from behind the counter. ''I need your help with a problem.''

Just in the ''nick'' of time, she thought. ''Coming.''

Nick sauntered toward the door. ''Later.''

Not if she could help it. She wouldn't put it past Nick to hound her about Luke...which would be just retribution for the hard time she always gave him.

Relieved at the reprieve, even a problematic one, Helen rounded the counter. ''What's up, Kate?''

''Something with the espresso maker.''

''What is it doing?''

"That's the problem. Not a thing."

Helen checked the equipment over herself. Kate was right. Nothing.

Suddenly feeling a little warm, Helen realized it wasn't embarrassment this time. "You know, the air-conditioning doesn't seem to be running, either." Though it did go off and on to keep the temperature level in the store, she had a bad feeling. They'd had electrical problems barely two weeks before. And now this... "Could be the main circuit. Let me go check the breaker box."

But it couldn't be the main circuit, she realized. The lights were still on and the computers were running. She hurried through the back room where a door exited into a small hallway. The breaker boxes, one for each floor, were located in the janitor's closet.

Indeed, some kind of power surge had switched off one of the breakers. Breathing a huge sigh of relief, Helen flipped it back on. But her relief was short-lived. When she returned to the café, she told Kate to turn the espresso machine back on, but nothing happened.

"Sorry, Helen, it's simply dead."

The air conditioner, however, chose that moment to go on and send a chill straight down Helen's spine.

"I don't understand. This machine isn't even a year old. How can it be dead?"

Kate shrugged. "Equipment breaks down. As my mother always says, they don't make things the way they used to."

If only that were true. If only she hadn't had a

string of bad things, including the talcum powder prank, happen to her in the space of a few weeks.

Putting aside her paranoia for the moment, she said, "Okay, I'll go in back and put in a call for a repair."

But her luck continued to run bad. No one was available to come out that day. What was she going to do now? Lunch hour was almost upon them.

"What are we going to do?" Kate asked. "Close for the day?"

"No!" If someone was messing with her business, she wouldn't give that person the satisfaction. But not Luke... Surely Luke couldn't have sabotaged her. "I guess we'll just have to serve regular coffee with a smile and hope we don't lose any more customers." Her mind raced for a way to compensate for disappointments. "Free coffee."

"Free?" Kate echoed.

"Right. I'll make up some signs apologizing for the temporary lack of fancy coffees. Offering a cup of regular or decaf coffee free should make most people happy."

Kate appeared as unhappy as Helen felt. Her assistant manager stared at the dead machine and shook her head.

And Helen tried to shake away the sense of doom. The repair person would be there the next day. But what if he didn't have the part? That could mean another day. Or what if the part had to be special ordered? That could mean disaster.

One day at a time, she told herself, though it was hard to fight her growing sense of doom.

Helen sat before one of the computers and made up a flyer offering free coffee.

What if she went out and bought another machine—a smaller, less expensive one? The hulk taking up her counter space had cost her nearly six thousand dollars. No, another machine was out of the question. She could bring in her personal machine, but it wouldn't come close to doing the job. Maybe she could rent one.

By the time lunch customers started coming in, Helen had posted the Free Coffee signs prominently in several places. Things went smoothly, with some of the regulars expressing sympathy for her plight, but giving her encouraging words for her generosity.

And then in the middle of the rush, a familiar and not-so-welcome redhead walked in.

"What? No espresso?" Flash Gordon raised her perfectly plucked eyebrows and spoke in a voice loud enough to be heard in the far reaches of the now busy café. "I can't believe this place doesn't have a backup system. This would *never* happen at Hot Zone."

Biting her tongue lest she say something sharp in front of her other customers, Helen tried to pretend the situation didn't bother her.

"Lucky we have loyal customers who understand things can go wrong in the best of businesses." Helen pasted on her most winning smile. "Now, what can I get you? Decaf?" Maybe that would bring the public relations woman down a notch.

"Thanks, but no thanks," Flash said. "If I can't

get what I want...well, I'll simply go elsewhere. Someplace more...reliable."

With that, Luke's employee swept out of the store. Unfortunately, several customers followed.

Helen tried to put Flash Gordon out of her mind, but the woman's too-convenient appearance in the middle of a rush sat there like a black cloud in Helen's mind. It was as if the public relations woman had a purpose in showing up. And she'd definitely seemed disappointed by the smooth way Helen had chosen to handle the crisis.

Because she'd been hoping for another outcome?

Had she *known?*

Somehow, they got through the lunch rush without any other disgruntled customer making a complaint.

Then, when the place was about empty, and Helen was about to collapse now that her adrenaline high was over, the bell over the door dinged. She turned to see Luke walk in and hold the door for someone behind him.

"This way," he said.

One guy wearing paint-splattered overalls backed through the door. Brow furrowing, Helen rounded the counter to see what was going on as a second workman followed. When she saw what they were carrying, she stopped dead.

"What's going on?"

Luke's gaze met hers and he gave her a slow, syrupy smile that shot butterflies through her stomach.

"Afternoon, darlin'," he said, his voice low, husky and even more thrilling than the equipment he was delivering to her door. "I heard you needed some rescuing."

LUKE PUT the espresso machine he'd brought over through its paces to make certain it was working properly. Hot Zone had two machines. This was the smaller one, the extra to be used on the busy weekends at the service station located at the bottom of the former swimming pool.

He made two Breves and handed one to Helen, whose green eyes held a touch of confusion.

"You're my hero."

He clinked cups with her. "We aim to please."

"Luke, this was so generous of you...."

"And you find it hard to believe that I'm helping the competition."

"Well..."

"I told you to trust me. There's room enough in this neighborhood for both of our cafés."

While Helen appeared relieved, she also seemed exhausted. Stress could do that to a person, as he well knew. And her day was not yet done.

"You could use a break," Luke said. He looked around. The last of the stragglers had left and, for the moment, the café was empty. "Why don't we get out of here for a little while? Some fresh air and sunshine would do you good."

"I wouldn't mind," Helen admitted, looking around. "Kate," she called. "Did you see where she went?" she asked Luke.

"Can't say that I did."

When he'd walked in that door, he hadn't noticed anyone but Helen. Then again, she was all he'd been thinking about since the night before. Well, pretty much since he'd made her acquaintance in the picket line.

Now she was looking puzzled and heading for the rear doorway. "Let me see if Kate's in back."

Luke watched her go. He was fascinated by her walk, by the way her body moved with an effortless sensuality, as if she was confident of herself without feeling like she had to prove it to everyone.

When she disappeared from view, he felt as if the room had dimmed, but of course that was his imagination.

The workmen had moved the broken espresso maker to the side of the preparation space. The cord was dangling, the plug lying on the floor. Luke grabbed hold of the cord, intending to wrap it up out of the way lest someone trip over it. And the problem became clear.

"Kate's in the rest room," Helen said, coming back, shoulder bag in hand.

"Hello." He held up the plug for Helen to see. "I think I found our problem."

She shrugged. "What?"

"The third prong. The ground is missing. I'm assuming you didn't know about this."

"No, of course not."

"All you needed was a good surge and the espresso machine got overloaded."

"What kind of surge?" she asked.

"If something else with a lot of power turned off, this baby would get the brunt of the extra power."

"Like an air conditioner going off when the store got cool enough."

"That might do it. But there's still the question of how this happened." He waggled the damaged plug.

"Got me. Who knows how long it's been that way? I've had a half-dozen different kids working here the past month. Maybe one of them had an accident. Or maybe it was the janitor. Whoever it was obviously didn't want to fess up and face the music."

Thinking she sounded like she was trying to convince herself, he said, "Which could be a pretty serious tune, depending on how much of the electronics got fried."

Helen groaned. "This doesn't seem to be my lucky month."

"Okay, I'm back," Kate said, moving behind the counter. "You two can hit the road, while I hold down the fort."

"We won't be long," Helen promised.

The employee's attention was already focused on the borrowed equipment, while Luke's attention was on getting Helen to himself.

Or at least out of the store and away from business.

The day was hot but not humid, so it was fairly comfortable in the shade. Luke suggested a short walk to a restaurant with outdoor seating. That gave him the opportunity to place an arm behind Helen's back as they crossed the street. His hand landed on the back of her other arm and he swore he felt her pulse jump at the contact.

"I missed you," he said, breathing in her scent.

"When did you have time to miss me?"

"I was awake half the night." He'd tortured himself imagining what she would be willing to do on their next date. Even thinking about it now gave him a hard-on. "Are you saying you didn't think about me at all?"

"I didn't say that."

"Well, then."

"So when you were thinking…what came to mind?"

"What our second date would be like. And this is not it. This is in the nature of a rescue mission."

"About that. How did you know? Did your wonderful Flash come back to Hot Zone gloating?"

"Flash? No. I was on my way to see you when I passed some of your customers talking about it, so I turned right around to get one of my machines. I didn't know Flash had set foot in your place."

"Not only today, but yesterday, too. She came for your assistant."

"Alexis?"

"Yeah, they were arguing about something."

"They're not real fond of each other," Luke said. "But usually they work in an atmosphere of tolerance. I was busy with a photographer and a reporter looking for a story. Any idea what the problem might have been?"

She shook her head. "I was at the computer. Anyway, today when Flash came in, she was...well, a little testy about not getting whatever it was she wanted.''

''A fancy coffee,'' he assumed.

''Hmm, I wonder.''

But they'd arrived at the restaurant and Luke didn't want to pursue a negative line of thought, so he didn't question her further. He wanted personal time with Helen that she couldn't count as a date.

Even so, Flash's showing up at the cybercafé just when things were going wrong sat at the back of his mind, competing with his alone time with Helen.

''I THOUGHT I would quit my job and run away with the postman,'' Christine Rhodes announced.

''Uh-huh,'' Helen murmured, then realized what her mother had just said. Movie credits were running on the television screen, so she used the remote to turn it off, then faced the woman parked at the other end of the couch. ''What? Surely you're not serious? You're in love with the postman?''

Her mother gave her an exasperated expression. ''Just checking to see if you were listening. You've been in your own world all night.''

Earlier, they'd sprawled out in her mom's living room and had shared Chinese takeout straight from the cartons while watching a pay-per-view movie, a long-standing once-a-month tradition that they both enjoyed. Normally, anyway. Tonight, Helen's mind had been otherwise occupied. She didn't even know how the movie had ended.

"Sorry, Mom, I don't mean to be bad company."

"But you'd rather be elsewhere."

Guiltily, Helen realized her thoughts had been centered on Luke and the temptation of a second date with him. She'd been fantasizing from the moment he'd dropped her back at the café after lunch. Not that they'd made plans. He'd asked what she was doing that evening, and she'd told him about her standing date with her mother.

Not wanting hurt feelings, Helen tried evading the issue. "You know I love our evenings together."

Her mother gave her an intense examination that sharpened her lovely features. Barely fifty and seeming a decade or so younger, Christine Rhodes was the epitome of the alluring older woman, from her sleek golden blond hair to her voluptuous figure, the same perfect ten it had always been. Most people seeing them together assumed they were sisters rather than mother and daughter.

Helen knew she was lucky to have inherited her mom's great genes.

And unlucky, too.

"What's his name?" Christine asked. "And don't put on that innocent act, either. My instincts and that soft expression you wore when you didn't know I was looking tell me it's a man who has your attention tonight."

"Whether I want him to or not," Helen admitted with a sigh. She swore there was nothing she could hide from her mom, a realization that had scared her since she was a kid.

"Is this man nice?"

"Charming."

"Good-looking?"

"Gorgeous."

"Among the employed?"

"Business owner and potential workaholic."

"Hmm, should be perfect for you," Christine said. "You do know his name, don't you?"

Helen cringed inside as she said, "Luke DeVries."

"DeVries?" Her mother sat up straighter at her end of the couch. "As in the owner of Hot Zone?"

"The very one."

The very one she'd told her mom about in the most unflattering of terms. But that had been before she'd actually met Luke.

"O-o-oh."

Helen said, "Just a week ago, I wanted in the worst way to drive him out of town…at least out of the neighborhood. And now, after meeting him and spending time with him…" She sighed again. "All I want…"

"Is him in your bed?"

"Mom!"

"Or is he already there?"

"Stop! This isn't the kind of thing you and I can talk about."

"And why not? We talk about everything else. I'm sure you've told Annie all about this Luke."

"Actually, I haven't." Not this time. This time she didn't seem to know what she was doing. Didn't feel in control of the situation…or of her own feelings.

"Besides, even if I had, Annie is my best friend, while you're my mother, for heaven's sake!"

"Well, the last I heard, that wasn't a crime," Christine huffed. She slid closer to her only child and wrapped motherly arms around Helen. "You think I've forgotten what it's like to be young? Or that I've forgotten how powerful sexual attraction can be? Don't count me out on that score yet, my darling daughter."

Helen made a face and sank deeper into her end of the couch. "Let's not go there," she pleaded, wondering why she couldn't have kept her mind where it belonged—in this room, not in the bedroom—for a few hours.

"I think we should have gone there a long time ago. You know you can talk to me about anything." Christine smoothed Helen's hair from her face as she said, "I've always gotten the feeling you avoid getting close to a man."

"Um, that's not exactly true."

"Okay, now I'm not talking about sex. I mean the kind of closeness that allows you to know what a man's thinking…a special man."

"I don't need that kind of closeness," Helen insisted, even as she thought of Luke again.

"Uh-huh."

Helen squirmed and felt as if the room had grown too hot. "I'm fine dating lots of men. I don't need to settle on just one."

"I'm not talking about settling. I'm talking about being madly in love with someone who loves you the same way. Someone who will put you ahead of himself."

"Yeah, right. Like they're lined up out there, waiting for the right woman to come along."

"You're afraid. That's only natural. But if you don't put yourself out there sometime..."

She'd end up like her mom. Alone. Not that Helen would say that aloud. She wouldn't hurt the one person who'd taken care of her all her life...who would do anything for her...who would always love her.

Squirming from her mother's arms, she rose. "Time for dessert. Any preference?"

"Butter pecan."

Helen rolled her eyes and headed for the kitchen, muttering, "Why do I bother to ask?"

Though the freezer was stocked with several flavors, her mother always chose the same one. She, on the other hand, indulged herself with a variety of tastes.

And a variety of men.

Tonight she felt like rum raisin. Taking the two pints from the freezer, she picked up a couple of spoons and napkins and headed back into the living room, where she tossed the pint of butter pecan to her mother.

She'd known since puberty how alike mother and daughter really were. Men flocked around the Rhodes women for what they could get...and then discarded them.

Helen reclaimed her place on the couch and they

sat there in silence, concentrating on their respective pints of ice cream.

Trophy women, both of them, mother and daughter, Helen thought. The Rhodes women were cursed by their looks.

They might both be alone, but while her mother had lived her life broken-hearted—her father having left her mother to marry another woman—Helen chose to keep her own heart intact.

Luke was obviously attracted to her. He wanted her for now. But in the end, he would be like the others and move on to someone more suitable, less threatening. Hell, he would move on to another town. And soon.

That's why she chose her men just like she chose her ice creams, she thought and scooped a heaping spoonful into her mouth.

7

LUKE SPENT the better part of the morning mired in last-minute details to make certain Hot Zone would be ready for Sunday's opening. Bringing the plumber back to fix a faucet that leaked in the men's locker room… Approving plans for the flower arrangements that would be delivered on Saturday afternoon…

Sending Alexis out to a local warehouse store to buy a supply of toilet paper and napkins when their shipment of paper products didn't come and she learned their order had somehow gotten lost.

And through the pandemonium, thoughts of Helen flitted in and out of his mind. Thoughts that were driving him crazy.

Get a grip, DeVries, he told himself.

He had more important things on his mind than his next encounter with a woman who seemed determined to push him right out of her life before he even got in.

Was that the attraction? he wondered as he left the café for his temporary headquarters, the suite of offices on the second floor, to check his messages. *Was Helen's playing hard to get turning him on?*

But she didn't do it with panache, he reasoned, not

like a woman who was so sure of herself she could snap her fingers and a man would come running. Though he wished she would snap her fingers at him.

And he was ready to snap back, he thought, grinning as he took the stairs two at a time. His imagination ran wild at the possibilities of where he could "snap" her.

He reached the office and settled down at the reception desk where he checked over several handwritten reminders of things to do. By that time Luke was envisioning nibbling Helen's stomach again, then her inner thighs.

What he wouldn't have done the night before for a second date. *Second date...touching.* And he would be more than ready to slide all the way home....

He was ready now.

Great. Now he had an erection with the hardness, if not the size, of a baseball bat.

The office door flew open. "Okay, one crisis averted."

"Alexis. And you're back so soon," he said, thankful for the desk between them.

"You told me to be quick about it."

"So I did. And you came through, as always. What would I ever do without you?"

"Let's hope you never have to find out," Alexis said, picking up the clipboard with the growing list of last-minute tasks.

"Problem?"

"Flash."

"She's been on your case?"

"Whenever possible. You would think this was her company, that *she's* the woman behind the man."

Luke started at the possessive tone he heard in her voice, at the way Alexis had emphasized the *she.* But his assistant didn't illuminate him further. Her forehead furrowed, she was looking down at the clipboard, her attention fixed.

"Okay, then," she muttered, setting down the list and heading for the door. "I'd better get busy or we won't be ready."

Luke stared after her. He hadn't been imagining it. Why hadn't he noticed before?

Alexis complained about Flash's proprietary attitude, yet she was every bit as invested in Hot Zone as was his public relations director.

The woman behind the man.

Did Flash really think of herself that way?

Or did Alexis?

"ALL DONE," the repairman said as he finished testing the espresso machine he'd just fixed. "Good as new. You want I should switch it with the one you borrowed?"

"That would be great," Helen said, taking the time to help him.

Luckily it was midafternoon and her only customers were a couple of regulars who'd already had their orders filled. Her own equipment was back in place and up and running before the next person walked through the door.

How was she ever going to thank Luke? she wondered.

She could think of plenty of ways…

''Okay, sign here,'' the repairman said, cutting into thoughts that had been on the road to lascivious.

Helen signed, ignoring the cost, simply glad to be back in business on her own.

The repairman picked up his tool case. ''See you.''

''Not too soon, I hope,'' Helen muttered. Making herself a cappuccino, she said, ''Kate, would you start cleaning Hot Zone's machine, while I call Luke and tell him we're back in business on our own?''

''You're the boss.''

Wanting a little privacy in case the call turned personal, Helen decided to use the phone in the back room, basically a combination storage area and office. She flopped down at the desk, found the Hot Zone office number and picked up the phone, then, not wanting to sound too eager, waited a moment to take a deep breath before using it.

Her pulse had picked up and she was getting a buzz at the mere thought of speaking to Luke. Her mouth was dry and the sweet spot between her thighs wasn't.

How unlike her, Helen thought. Then again, Luke wasn't like any other man she'd dated.

Squeezing her knees together and telling her emotions to behave, she tapped in the number and took another deep breath as the phone rang on the other end.

But when it picked up, she was disappointed to

hear a female voice say, "Hot Zone. Alexis Stark here."

"Luke DeVries, please."

"Can I ask who's calling?"

"Helen Rhodes."

"Sorry, Ms. Rhodes, he's not available right now."

Helen couldn't miss the way the other woman's voice grew tight, her words clipped. A little uneasy, she asked, "When will he—"

"I really couldn't say," Alexis said, cutting her off sharply. "We're up to our eyebrows in last-minute details for the opening."

As if she didn't know that.

"It's about the espresso machine Luke so kindly lent me," Helen said in a tone that was friendlier than she was feeling. "The repairman just left, so your machine is freed up. Maybe you could tell Luke that, ask him to call me."

"I'll send a couple of guys over to pick up our equipment. No need to bother Luke about some little errand."

"But I want to thank him—"

"I'll personally thank him for you," Alexis said, now sounding exasperated. "And someone will be at your place within the next hour."

"Tell Luke—"

Again her words were cut off, but this time by Alexis hanging up. Helen could hardly believe the young woman's rudeness.

Hanging up herself, she sat there for a moment, wondering if she had reason to be upset. Was Alexis trying to come between them or were her emotions so screwed around that she was seeing problems where there were none? Of course they were busy. Probably harried. And she might have interrupted Alexis at a bad time.

Figuring that had to be it, she decided to get back to business. Kate was just finishing cleaning the Hot Zone equipment when Helen joined her behind the counter.

"So how soon will Luke be here?"

"Luke won't be making a personal appearance today. His assistant said she would send someone over to fetch the espresso machine."

Kate shrugged. "He's probably too busy right now. His grand opening is only three days away."

"Right."

Though Helen hadn't known Kate was counting, her assistant manager had probably bought into her own stress over the opening. After all, if Helen's Cybercafé was driven out of business, Kate would be out of a job.

"With that kind of man, business comes before anything else," Kate said, as she took ceramic cups out of the dishwasher and lined them up on the back counter. "His identity is all wrapped up in Hot Zone."

"You seem to know an awful lot about the competition."

Kate flushed. "How could I not when the competition has had such great media coverage around here in the past week?"

"That's true."

Some of it at her expense, Helen remembered. And undoubtedly she presented a conundrum to Kate, what with her dating the owner of the Hot Zone right after she'd organized a protest against his business.

Kate said, "I'm sure he'll call you, though, once he gets his equipment back."

"I'm sure," Helen echoed, hoping against hope that Luke would actually come in person anyway.

She ought to have been working on the Muscle Beach Web site, but focusing seemed to be a problem. Horrified at herself, she realized she was watching the door in hopes that Luke DeVries would walk through at any minute. Customers came in and went out but no Luke. An hour passed, the workmen arriving as promised. Even though the equipment was on its way back to Hot Zone, a tiny hope lingered.

And then business picked up and the commuter rush smothered any thoughts other than keeping customer orders straight.

By the time the evening crush settled down to an occasional patron, and Helen could join a newly arrived Annie for a fresh cappuccino, she was wondering if Luke had changed his mind about wanting to see her.

"Nick is really nervous about his video premiere tomorrow night," Annie said.

"Uh-huh."

"Something about Isabel seeing his work."

"Oh."

"Not that she hasn't seen it before," Annie went

on, Helen hearing her through a haze, "but I guess there's something special about this footage."

"I guess."

Vaguely remembering Nick had been editing footage of Isabel and her sister Louise made Helen wonder again about what it would be like to have that kind of special relationship with a man. What it would be like *not* to be the fifth wheel for once. She was always the odd person out since she rarely introduced her dates to her friends, let alone double-dated with them.

"Earth to Helen."

"What?" Focusing, Helen connected with Annie's puzzled gaze.

"I feel like you're on another planet."

Remembering her mother's similar complaint the night before, Helen flushed. "Sorry. I've got that Muscle Beach Web site to finish and—"

"You weren't thinking about any Web site."

"I *should* be thinking about the Web site."

"But you're thinking about Luke."

"Guilty."

"When are you seeing him again?" Annie asked.

Helen shrugged.

"Is that the problem? What are you doing about it? Why don't you simply call him and find out?"

"I did. Well, I called about business—his espresso machine—but his assistant said she'd handle it and wouldn't let me talk to him because he was too busy."

"So call his cell."

"If only he'd given me the number."

"This isn't like you," Annie admonished. "Man, you're so itchy you're sending out vibes."

"Itchy?" When Annie's eyebrows jutted up above her glasses, Helen said, "Oh."

"Luke DeVries must be some scratching post."

"I wouldn't exactly know about that." Though they hadn't done the deed yet, imagining the experience was enough to make her knees weak. Not wanting to give her sharp friend too much fuel, she resorted to her best weapon. "But he's something, all right. I just don't know if they've given it a name yet."

"Sarcasm won't put me off. Or him."

"From your lips…"

"You mean from his lips. You really do have it bad. Nick was right."

Moaning, Helen muttered, "Nick? Right about something? I'm doomed."

HELEN WASN'T FEELING quite so dramatic later that night as she sat alone pretending to watch bad television and thinking maybe she ought to get herself a cat. Then, at least, even if it wasn't sexual, she'd have someone to talk to and cuddle up with at night.

No, with her luck, she'd probably pick a cat who would be perverse enough to sit at the end of the bed and snicker at her foolishness.

Maybe she could read.

She'd just turned off the television, put on some music and was looking through the fashion magazines piled up on an end table, when her doorbell buzzed. It was after nine and she wasn't expecting anyone. Unless Annie had talked to Nick and he'd decided to drop by to torture her.

A cautious city girl, Helen didn't simply open the door. First she checked to see who was outside.

The bell rang again.

Yikes! Luke!

And from his expression under the porch light, he knew she was there. She wore a pair of stretch pants and a big T-shirt for comfort. Her face was clean of makeup, her hair clipped back, away from her face. And she was barefoot.

But there was simply no helping it—she had to open the door.

She opted for opening it a crack. "Luke, hi," she said, hiding behind as much door as possible, hoping that with her foyer light off he couldn't possibly see her well enough to be disenchanted. She could see him, though, gorgeous and well groomed as usual. "What are you doing here?"

"Hello, darlin'. I wanted to talk to you and took the chance you'd be home. Can I come in?"

"Well, uh…"

He started. "Sorry. What was I thinking, assuming you would be alone."

"I am alone." And trapped now that she'd confirmed it. Damn! She stepped back. "Come on in."

"You're sure?"

Luke must have felt her answering glare, for he rushed in. Or maybe he was simply taking the opportunity before she could change her mind. Helen locked the door and followed him into the living room, lit only by the two lamps she used when watching television.

"Your espresso machine is okay, right?" she asked, stopping at the nearest couch.

"I guess." He gave her a puzzled look. "Oh, then yours is fixed."

"Yes. You didn't know yours came back? You didn't get my thank-you?"

"No and no."

"Great."

"When did all this happen?"

"This afternoon. I wanted to talk to you personally, but your assistant wouldn't call you to the phone. I realize how busy you all must have been, but I wish she had at least passed on my thank-you. I wouldn't want you to think I wasn't grateful."

"I'm sure Alexis simply forgot," Luke said with a shrug. "One crisis after another needed solving or I would have called you earlier anyway."

"And yet you didn't call at all."

"I wanted to see you."

The sound of his voice when he said it was so sexy, it took Helen's breath away. She swallowed hard and her pulse picked up as she said, "A little late for a date, don't you think?"

"Not a date. Just...see you. Maybe have that cup of coffee and get to know each other a little better."

"*Now* you want coffee?"

"What? You don't have any in the house? I could go out and get whatever—"

"Enough. Okay, a visit. Coffee. Get to know one another better. It's a plan."

"So which way to the kitchen?"

"No one invited you," Helen said, whisking by him and across the room. "I know how to make coffee, too, you know." She glanced back at him. "It's late. Decaf?"

He shook his head and smiled so that dimple kissed his cheek. "Give me everything you've got."

Now why did he make that sound like something more personal than coffee?

"I'll certainly give it my best shot." She indicated the table where the fashion magazines lay. "You can wait here and read or turn on the TV or—"

"I know how to amuse myself."

He was looking at her in a way that made her catch her breath.

Helen turned and nearly ran into the kitchen.

Coffee...coffee...but what kind?

It had to be special. Had to wow him. Had to out-orgasm his Orgasm, she thought, remembering the special brew he'd whipped up for her.

While the water was heating, she got her other ingredients together on the counter.

And then she ran into the powder room where she unclipped her hair and finger-combed it into a wild mess which she hoped looked sexy. A swipe of pale lip gloss and then she was back in the kitchen mixing ingredients.

Several minutes later, she carried a tray with two large cups into the living room, where Luke was looking over her CD collection.

"See anything you like?" she asked.

He glanced back at her. "Very much."

"I meant the music."

"Enigma does it for me," he said of the selection playing at the moment.

They sat on the same couch with room to spare between them.

Luke eyed the oversize cups. "That should keep me running half the night."

"It's not all caffeine. There's Godiva liqueur and some Chambord—"

"Chocolate and raspberry. Very sensual combination."

"—and fresh raspberries steamed in the heavy cream."

"A woman after my own heart."

Was she?

Helen concentrated on her own cup, stirring the concoction once before tasting it. She watched him over the rim of her cup. A connoisseur, he swirled his drink, took a sip and looked as if he were analyzing it.

"Outstanding."

Helen let go of the breath she didn't know she'd been holding. His approval was more important to her than she would have guessed.

"So what did you want to talk about?" she asked, guessing it had to do with their next date.

Luke took another sip and surprised her. "I thought you'd like to know I called Peggy."

"You called your little sister? That's great!" she said, then hesitated. "Right?"

"Right. She was all excited, and here I never realized she even thought about me."

Speaking from experience, from the buried longing over the siblings who refused to acknowledge her existence, Helen said, "I bet she thinks about you a lot."

He nodded. "Thank you."

"For?"

"Making me realize what a dolt I've been for too many years. I promised to visit her when all the furor with the new store dies down."

A reminder that he would be leaving town all too soon, Helen thought. "Good for you."

"You're right. Developing a relationship with my little sister *will* be good for me. Now I have to try to figure out what a thirteen-year-old likes to do."

"It'll come back to you. Like riding a bike."

"Or I could use help."

He was looking at her pointedly, making her pulse jump.

"I'll see what I can come up with."

Luke took another sip of the coffee. "You should patent this stuff before someone steals it from you."

The offhand remark gave her a different kind of jolt, reminded her that they would soon be in competition. She had to keep that in mind, Helen thought.

"What do you call it?" he asked.

"No need to name it. I can't serve this at the cybercafé. No liquor license."

"I don't suppose trying to get one would make sense since you close early." Suddenly switching gears, he asked, "So what are you doing tomorrow night?"

Her pulse suddenly picked up and her mouth went dry. Helen called herself a fool. How could one little question have such an effect?

"Tomorrow? I've made plans with my friends," she said, remembering Nick's video. "But you could join us. Annie and Nate and I are going to Club Undercover with Nick and his lady Isabel. Nick shoots and edits videos for the club, and they're showing a new cut tomorrow night."

"Great. I'll get to spend some time with your friends, then."

He made it sound like there was a reason to get to know them, when really there wasn't, she told herself.

As if he could hear her thoughts, Luke said, "I envy you. I've never stayed in one place long enough to make friendships that would last a lifetime."

Again he was reminding her of their short future together. Soon he would be off and running, conquering yet another city. So what was she doing, sharing time with him, when they could be alone?

Too late to change her mind now, though.

"It'll be fun," she promised, trying to beat back the unsettled feeling that suddenly gripped her.

"You look a little tired."

"Long day."

''Then I should go,'' Luke said, setting down his cup.

He didn't get to his feet, though, and from the way he locked gazes with her, Helen had the feeling he had something else in mind totally. When he started to move closer, she put out her hand to stay him.

''Not even a kiss?'' he asked softly.

Longing for the feel of his lips on hers—on other parts of her—she said, ''This isn't a date, remember.''

If he insisted, she would be too weak to hold out. But she didn't want tomorrow night to be date number three. She wanted to draw out this…this…well, whatever they had going between them…for as long as possible.

''Close your eyes,'' Luke said.

''But—''

''I'll close mine, then you close yours.''

What was he up to now? she wondered as his long, thick lashes fluttered downward to tease his high cheekbones.

Following suit, she said, ''Don't think that just because your eyes are closed a kiss doesn't count.''

''Even if we don't actually touch?''

''Huh?''

Her eyes popped open but his were still closed and he hadn't so much as inched closer. Telling herself to relax was futile, but she did close her eyes again.

''What now?''

''Now we imagine it. Our lips touching…your mouth opening to mine…wet warmth…my tongue sliding inside…''

Warmth sizzled through her and Helen shifted, seeking relief from the sweet discomfort. "And then what?"

"What do you want to have happen?"

"I don't know."

"You must. You've been thinking about this all day."

"What makes you so sure?"

"Because I have. What next?" he repeated.

"Another kiss."

"That's all you want?"

"All right. Your hand stroking my cheek… following the line of my throat…finding my breast…"

"What do I do to it?" When she didn't answer, he said, "I slip my hand under its fullness and feel its weight…my thumb finds your nipple and teases it into a hard peak…and then you touch me…."

She could see it…feel it all…just as if it were happening.

"You're so hard," she whispered, mentally running her fingers over his length to the tip where she discovered a tiny drop of fluid and spread it over the head. "I love touching you, but I want to taste you."

"Go ahead. Put your mouth around me."

Helen licked her lips as though she were preparing to give him head. She could feel him in her mouth, could taste him. She thought about taking him deeper, relaxing the back of her throat until she could feel his head probing there.

"Mmm, feels so good," Luke murmured. "Now

I'm tangling my hands in your hair and pulling it back because I want to see everything."

"Yes, watch," she said breathlessly.

Luke opened his eyes and if he didn't already have a hard-on, one look at Helen would have done it. She was laying back against the couch, her legs spread slightly. Her hand was on her stomach, near the vee between her thighs, fingers pointed downward as if she wanted to touch herself. He imagined she was wet, so wet that her fingers would slide right up...

"Touch yourself," he said.

"What?"

"Don't talk with your mouth full," he teased, his voice tight. "Your mouth is on me and your hand is on yourself...exploring...leaving trails of sensation everywhere."

He watched as her fingers dipped lower and her breath caught in her throat when she touched herself intimately, and he thought he might come right then, right there, without her ever touching him at all.

What the hell was he doing? This woman made him crazy with wanting her and once more he would go to bed with a boner. But she was so naturally sexy, so open about it, he couldn't help but say and do things he would never even think of with another woman.

Helen Rhodes had some kind of hold on him.

Startled by that reality—he was used to being in control—Luke took a deep breath as she softly moaned and his body responded to the sound. Her fingers had disappeared between her thighs.

"Now what?" she asked.

For a moment, he was tempted to tell her, to detail every move he wanted them both to make. He wanted to watch her skin flush...wanted to see her wet her lips and bite them...wanted to hear her moan as sensation swept her...wanted to be privy to her coming as she masturbated.

But something held him back.

The brain might be the best sex toy ever, but he didn't want a toy. He didn't want to play. He was serious about wanting the gritty, sweaty reality of tumbling on her, thrusting into her and maybe even coming all over her. He wanted to touch her, to taste her, to take her until she was mindless with need.

He didn't want fantasy.

But obviously she did or she wouldn't have created some dumb rules for dating that somehow shielded her from the realities of having a healthy sex life.

Why? What had happened to her? What was she afraid of?

Now wasn't the time to shatter whatever illusions she was under. He couldn't do that to her. Instead he simply wanted to be kind to her, something he'd never been particularly good at with women.

"Now we kiss again," he murmured, looking away so that he could end this gracefully. "We kiss and hold each other and savor the magic that we know will come."

8

"So help me, Nick," Helen said during their morning coffee get-together, "you'd better not try to embarrass me in front of Luke tonight or—"

"Or you'll what?" he challenged her.

"Or I'll tell Isabel about...about *the thing*."

"No, not *the thing!*" he said in mock horror.

"*What* thing?" Annie asked.

"Nick knows," Helen hedged, making this up as she went along. "The thing that happened in college."

In reality, Nick could do whatever he pleased to embarrass her, and she couldn't do squat to stop him.

"A *thing* happened?" Annie glared at them suspiciously. "Why don't I know about it?"

Both Helen and Nick gave Annie looks of sympathy, as if confirming they'd been correct in assigning her to the status of "innocent" long ago.

"Oh, cut it out! You two—I'm surprised you two didn't kill one another long ago. Maybe that would have been a *good* thing," Annie muttered to herself.

Nick said, "Helen talks a good game, but she's full of hot air, and I could take her if she tried anything."

Helen laughed. Nothing could dampen her spirits this morning, not even Nick Novak.

Annie rolled her eyes and rose. "Enough of this nonsense. Time to get to work. Are you coming?" she asked Helen.

Helen pushed out of her chair.

"You're going somewhere?" Nick asked.

"Just over to Annie's Attic."

He whistled. "Does Luke DeVries know he's going to get lucky tonight?"

"Don't get ahead of yourself," Helen warned him. "It's only the second date."

And before Nick could think of some zinger to irritate her, Helen made her escape.

Annie's Attic was on the Damen Avenue side of the triangular building, right below Nick's business. Helen gazed at the front window—Annie was famous for her sexy displays of her product. Today, her mannequin couple stood on what looked like a darkened elevated platform, the man behind the woman. He was pressing himself up against her and her low-rise jeans and half-open blouse revealed glimpses of jewel-tone undergarments.

Uh-oh, what had Annie and Nate been up to lately? Helen wondered, knowing the window often followed their sexual exploits.

She followed her friend into the store, a deep rose cave whose corners were draped with gold-shot cream swaths cascading from rings on the ceiling. Midnight-blue and vanilla-cream satin sheets filled the shelves on one wall, bottles and pots of potions and creams the other. She stopped to check out the racks of teddies and other delicate garments in jewel tones like those in the display. But she'd seen all these before.

"So what's new in the store?" Helen asked.

"Mood underwear," Annie told her, indicating another display. "The material starts out in one of these nice pastel colors, but if you get...well...in the mood...it becomes transparent so it looks like you're nude."

Did she dare? Helen wondered. *Second date, second stage.* Nearly anything went. Or would with Luke in charge. He had a creative style that she couldn't resist. And why should she? Their fling would be over soon enough. She considered the mood underwear. He'd play within her rules, but he would drive her crazy.

And she would love it and want more.

Her turn to have the upper hand, she thought. She could only imagine Luke's reaction if she allowed him to get far enough to see these flimsy garments.

Or not see them, as the case may be.

Contemplating the consequences was delicious, Helen admitted.

And highly irresistible.

SEEING HELEN in a different light the night before had Luke in a mood. He hadn't slept well, but not because he'd been horny. Once he'd backed off on the fantasy, his sexual excitement had faded fast, replaced by more serious considerations. Serious considerations about Helen Rhodes.

Ridiculous. He hardly knew the woman. Hadn't even slept with her yet. So what was his deal? What was making him stop and think about her at odd moments in the day when he should have been totally focused on his grand opening?

He looked around the office guiltily, as if someone would be watching him and realize he hadn't been working. Thankfully, he was alone for the moment.

Except for Helen-in-his-head, of course.

Why did he want to climb inside *her* head?

She was a real knockout on the outside and, despite a sometimes prickly nature, equally lovely on the inside. She was passionate, but she was also vulnerable, and as much as he liked the idea of making love to Helen, he wasn't sure he liked the idea of being vulnerable. He'd always opted for safe, never staying in one place long enough to do damage, and he wasn't about to start taking chances now.

But he didn't want to avoid Helen.

And what kind of damage was he worried about? he asked himself. Was he actually afraid of hurting a woman who wore her ridiculous dating rules like a protective skin?

Or was he afraid that *he* would want more this time and she wouldn't let him have it?

Luke recognized something of himself in Helen, something he didn't usually think about. But he was thinking now, mostly about how he avoided relationships to avoid disappointment later. He was more than thinking about it, thanks to her. He'd taken a first step toward a relationship with Peggy. He'd actually called

GET A Free MYSTERY GIFT…
We can't tell you what it is…but we're sure you'll like it! A FREE gift just for giving the Harlequin Reader Service® Program a try!
Visit us online at
www.eHarlequin.com

her and made plans to see the little sister he'd otherwise only remembered at Christmas and on her birthday.

Helen's siblings didn't even recognize her as being one of them. Their loss, as far as he was concerned. And he didn't want Peggy to feel abandoned as Helen did.

But Helen had friends in plenty, and maybe that drew him to her, as well. He wanted to know the secret of her success in that department—having people stick around because they really liked her, not because she provided them with a job or service. He was woefully lacking in that department. His father's military career had made it impossible for him to keep up long-term friendships, and he'd never learned how.

''Photo op time,'' Flash said as she swung into the office, startling Luke to sit up straight and take notice.

''Here? Now?'' he asked.

''Tonight.'' The woman's red hair practically sizzled with electricity when she said, ''A political fundraiser for the mayor,'' as though it were some fabulous opportunity.

''How in the world do you get that'll be a photo op for *us?*'' Luke wanted to know.

Not that he was interested. Not tonight.

Flash parked herself on the edge of his desk and crossed one shapely leg over the other. ''Everyone who is anyone will be there.''

''Except for me.''

''No, no, you have to be there. I was planning on

picking you up at nine. The party starts at eight so we'll be fashionably late—''

''Or would be if I didn't have other plans.''

A statement that stopped her dead in her tracks. Her eyebrows shot up. ''Other plans? Doing what, may I ask? No one told me.''

''I didn't think I had to check with you before going out with a friend.''

''A date?'' She pronounced the word with contempt. ''You've got to be kidding. We're opening on Sunday. That's forty-eight hours from now.''

''No one is more aware of that than I am, Flash.''

But he'd been living and breathing business for so long that he was getting sick of it being his whole life.

''Then what are you thinking? You need as much exposure as possible to make this new venue a success.''

''We both know how grueling the opening will be.''

But going to a political fund-raiser or a fund-raiser of any kind wasn't going to get him the customers who would be drawn to his business. What was Flash thinking? She was seriously bent out of shape. For a moment, Luke wondered if she had plans for herself that required her to be at that fund-raiser. If so, he wouldn't stand in her way.

''If you think you can work this party to our benefit, be my guest,'' Luke said. ''But, personally, I need a break. I need some downtime.''

What he needed was Helen, not that he would say that to his public relations director.

''I know you're a man and you need certain...distractions,'' Flash said with forced good humor, ''but this is not the time to go gooey-eyed over some blond airhead.''

So Flash knew he was seeing Helen. He hadn't been aware that she'd noticed.

''Helen Rhodes is no airhead,'' he said, keeping his temper in check. ''Don't underestimate her.''

''Don't *you* underestimate her, Luke. She staged that protest, remember. How do you know she isn't using you? She's probably seeing you to get information to ruin the Hot Zone opening.''

''The subject is closed,'' Luke said, trying to ignore his irritation.

Flash slid off his desk. ''Not as far as I'm concerned, it's not.''

''Who I choose to see privately is no concern of yours.''

''Hot Zone is my concern,'' she argued. ''It's my priority and it should be yours, as well.''

''Get off my back!'' Luke finally snapped.

Flash went pale and her eyes rounded. Apparently she got the message, because she didn't continue the argument. Instead, she turned on her spiked heel and stormed toward the door and past a bemused Alexis, who apparently had been standing there for some time, taking it all in.

His assistant glanced back, as if to watch Flash for a moment.

"Convinced?" was all she murmured to him before going to her desk and getting to work.

Alexis had warned him about Flash's proprietary attitude, but this was the first time Luke had experienced the seriousness of the problem for himself.

HELEN FELT like she'd tried on every possible item in her wardrobe before settling on a sari skirt that hung low on her hips—a gold-shot patchwork of magenta and teal—and an embroidered teal silk top that stopped just below her breasts. Both wrists were heavy with bracelets—some inset with sparkling gemstones—that jangled when she walked.

Her goal was to look like a prettily wrapped present that Luke couldn't resist unwrapping....

She was just slipping into a pair of strappy sandals when her doorbell rang. Her pulse shot up and warmth flushed her face. Grabbing her bag—a sparkly little number that didn't hold much more than her lipstick, keys and ID—she raced down to the first floor.

The bell rang again and she forced herself to slow down, to take a moment to compose herself so that she wouldn't look so eager. Feeling more in control, she opened the door.

One look at Luke, however, and Helen's insides flew out of control. Dressed in khaki pants and a white knit T-shirt topped with a navy blue sports jacket, a Rolex around one wrist, Luke was so gorgeously *GQ* that it almost hurt to look at him.

"Wow!" she gasped at the same time his eyebrows

shot up and his lips puckered into an admiring whistle.

Helen laughed.

"What's so funny, darlin'?"

"Us. We're a regular mutual admiration society."

They stood there, staring at each other for a moment, the connection between them thick with a tension that Helen couldn't put to anything but pure lust.

If it weren't for Nick's video they wouldn't be going anywhere.

"We'd better get going," she murmured, pulling the door shut behind her and locking it before she could weaken further.

When she turned, it was to see a cell phone in Luke's hand.

"I walked over here. Didn't want to drink and drive, so I thought a taxi was in order."

"To go four blocks? We can walk it in ten minutes."

"If that's your pleasure..." He tucked the cell into an inner pocket of his suit jacket.

"We'll get back to the pleasure part later," Helen murmured as she glided past him.

"Promise?"

BUMPER-TO-BUMPER cars lined this stretch of Milwaukee Avenue, their drivers searching for those elusive parking spaces. Most of the shops were closed, but the ones that were still open—an ear-piercing and tattooing parlor, and a comic-book store along with the restaurants and bars—were all overflowing with customers. And the closer they got to Club Undercover, the more the sidewalk became crowded with people.

He'd chosen the right neighborhood, Luke thought, knowing foot traffic would bring him enough customers to make this newest Hot Zone a success. He looked around at the people on the street, from young men and women of various means holding hands or flirting with each other...to an older man and younger woman alighting from a limo...to the homeless *Streetwise* vendor hawking his newspaper to people with more guilt than money to burn.

Aware of the woman at his side, Luke decided he'd chosen the right neighborhood because it was also hers.

He slid a hand around Helen's waist, his fingers meeting bare flesh above the low-hung skirt. She glanced up at him with a smile on her lips and a yearning in her gaze, and for a moment he forgot to breathe.

"We're here," she said, passing through the cave-like opening to stairs that led to the subterranean-level entrance. "Nick said to enter from the VIP door."

"Ah, I love a woman with clout."

A bouncer guarded the door. Probably six-five, head shaved, coffee skin glowing with the humidity, he was a force to be reckoned with. But when they approached, his dark face immediately lit with an easy smile.

"Hey, good to see you, baby," he said to Helen.

"You, too, Par-Tee. I hope Nick left my name on your list."

"Even if he didn't, you know I would let *you* in."

He opened the door, and with a flourish of his meaty hand, bade them enter.

Luke couldn't help but feel as if the man's intent gaze was glued to him, as if he were silently commanding him to do right by the woman he was accompanying.

Or maybe his imagination was running away with him, Luke thought, as he followed her inside and past the bar where a waitress in a sparkly blue dress lifted a tray of drinks.

Helen's friends were already there, gathered around a table front and center. And suddenly Luke's mouth went dry and his palms felt wet with sweat, and he only half heard the introductions.

"...Nick Novak, our host, and his lady, Isabel Grayson...and you know Annie Wilder, of course...her fiancé, Nate Bishop..."

Was he imagining it, or were they all staring at him, taking his measure, making sure he was good enough for their Helen, just as Par-Tee had.

That's what real friends did, he thought. They circled the wagons and protected each other's back when trouble was on the horizon.

All through the introductions, through the opening and pouring of champagne, through the toasts to Nick, Luke smiled and nodded and felt utterly removed.

The outsider pretending to fit in.

"NOT MANY MEN could get Helen all atwitter the way you have," Nick told Luke as he refilled champagne glasses.

And Helen silently vowed to make her friend suffer for his evil ways.

"Atwitter?" Luke asked, sounding like a hollow version of himself.

"Revved up. Count yourself as the first man she's ever picketed."

"Oh, that."

"What did you think I meant?" Nick asked, his expression a study in innocence.

"Nicky, honey, I don't think he understands your...uh...brand of humor," Isabel said.

"He'll get used to it," Nick promised. "He has to if he's going to be around Helen and me."

Isabel nodded. "True."

And then to Luke he said, "Helen's obviously reconsidered her opinion about the owner of Hot Zone, so we all will, too."

"Hear! Hear!" Annie said, grinning from ear to ear.

And Helen hoped that was it. If her friends made Luke too uncomfortable, they might scare him off. After all, it wasn't like they were in a relationship.

"Just know that we're all behind Helen," Nate injected, his expression serious. "Though if you passed muster with Helen without having to go through fire...well, you're a lucky man."

Nate's expression was far too serious for the occasion, and his obvious concern made Helen's cheeks grow warm. She'd given Nate such a hard time when he'd been pursuing Annie. Her suspicious nature had questioned his every move, and Annie had eventually picked up on it. The couple was solid now, and Nate didn't hold anything against her, thank goodness.

Suddenly the deejay's voice blasted over the speakers. "'Yours Forever' Enrique Iglesias, and new video footage by our own Nick Novak."

At their table, Nick raised his glass and said, "Here we go. This new video is dedicated to the woman I love. To you, Isabel, sweetheart."

"What? Nick, why didn't you say something before this?"

The normally cool-looking blonde flushed at Nick's words, but Helen could see that Isabel was pleased. And why not when the man she loved had done something so special for her?

"Because I wanted to surprise you." Nick gave her a quick kiss.

"To Isabel," everyone toasted as the lights lowered and the romantic song oozed through the airwaves. A close-up of Isabel's face faded in on the large screen behind the crowded dance floor, as well as on the monitors scattered throughout the club.

Normally Nick compiled and computerized video images that he'd shot around the city, images that could be run at random by computer behind any number of songs that didn't already have a dance video. But Helen knew that this project was special and that he'd synched the footage with this specific song. She saw him reach for Isabel's hand, saw the look they exchanged, saw Nick's homage to his lady.

Across the table, Nate was sliding a hand out of sight. Knowing that he and Annie delighted in taking chances, in "playing" in public, Helen quickly looked away only to be caught by Luke's gaze.

They stared at each other, and for a moment she wondered what was off. Then his gaze softened and seared her and she felt herself flush.

As she turned her attention back to the video and the images that made her ache with something she couldn't define, Luke's hand lightly grasped hers. Helen swallowed hard and gave him a quick squeeze in return. His fingers nudged at hers and she opened them so they could thread together.

For once she didn't feel like a fifth wheel.

So why did that scare her so?

SHE CHOSE A SPOT where she could see the entrance, but where someone arriving would have to know she was there to spot her. Then she settled down to wait for Luke to arrive. But as fifteen minutes stretched into twenty and forty and then nearly an hour, and she began to wonder if they meant to show at all, her patience dwindled to nothing.

What they might be doing instead of clubbing didn't bear consideration. She wasn't going to drive herself crazy with thoughts of Luke having sex with that woman.

At least sexual satisfaction would be all their joining would mean to him, she thought smugly. He'd had enough women over the years, but none of them had ever lasted. Not like she had. She tried to take comfort in that.

Impatiently, she checked her watch.

Nearly an hour and a half now. Damn! She was wasting her time.

But then, just as she was about to get up and leave, she spotted them coming down the metal spiral staircase that led from the private VIP section to the dance floor.

She should have known.

Of course Luke DeVries was a VIP. Her *own* very important person.

So why didn't she feel better just seeing him? Look at him, so relaxed, so sure of himself…so glued to every word spoken by the woman at his side. It disgusted her! And when he took Helen Rhodes in his arms and slow-danced her to the center of the crowd, his hands wandering down her back, touching every inch of flesh he could, her own stomach clenched.

That should be *her* out there in his arms. He should be looking down at *her* as if he were entranced. *She* should be the one driving him mad with desire.

Maybe if Helen was out of the way…

9

THE NEON LIGHT and music and raucous crowd faded into the background and all that was left was them in each other's arms. Helen snuggled up to Luke and decided to close her eyes and let her fantasies soar.

Through a euphoric haze, she saw them clinking glasses surrounded by candlelight...walking hand in hand through a forest preserve...shopping in a gourmet market and filling a single basket...experiencing every activity couples enjoyed, except for sex.

Her eyes popped open and it took her a minute to reorient herself. Her heart beat so hard she swore she could hear it rush through her head.

What in the world was wrong with her?

Why wouldn't her mind cooperate, get down and dirty the way she wanted?

Helen's mouth went dry and her body felt cold with sweat. The last fantasy in the world she should be indulging in was having a relationship with any man, and *this* man in particular.

The very thought made her want to choke. She wasn't going to allow herself to enter *that* trap. She was simply feeling sentimental after seeing Nick's homage to the woman who had become everything to him.

She didn't need that in her life.

All she needed was a little sex. And soon.

Helen pulled herself together, and leaning in to inhale Luke's very manly scent, she forced her mind to more prurient interests by remembering things he'd done to her already. Her body followed the path cleared by her mind and, before she knew it, she was getting into second-date mode.

Sighing in relief, Helen melted against Luke and tucked her forehead against his cheek. In return, he pulled her closer and splayed a hand across the base of her spine, his fingers meeting the bare flesh just above her low-slung skirt. Then his fingertips wandered downward, probing their way beneath the material, and Helen's pulse trilled from head to toes.

That was more like it!

She imagined the glorious things he could do to her with those fingers, one at a time or all together. And with his mouth, she thought with a smile. And with his…no, this was only their second date. She wouldn't go there, not yet.

But apparently Luke was already there. His erection pressed against the hollow between her thighs. Each small movement along the dance floor rubbed his hardened shaft against her sensitive flesh, the series of minute strokes quickly setting her on sexual edge. Her nipples tightened and wet warmth pooled between her thighs and she longed to be alone with him.

An exquisite torture.

They might as well have been having sex.

When the slow number ended, Helen pulled herself free of Luke's arms. "All right, then," she murmured, "let's get back upstairs."

"What's the hurry?" Luke murmured as the next selection, a slow and sultry number, began.

He reached for her, but she skittered away from him and headed for the winding metal staircase. Luke followed, pressing up against her back. He still had a hard-on. For a moment, she stopped and pressed back against him. His answering groan whispered through her hair, sending gooseflesh careening down her neck.

Knees suddenly weak, Helen moved to the side, saying, "You first," not wanting Luke behind her all the way up the stairs.

Eyebrows raised, he brushed by her and ran a hand along her tush, making her knees go even weaker. Taking a deep calming breath, hoping to be in complete control of herself by the time they got back to the table, she followed him up the winding metal staircase...one step at a time.

Nearly halfway up, her heel caught on something, and when she tried to free it, her foot wrenched sideways, throwing her off balance.

Even as she flew backward, Helen grabbed onto the rail with one hand to stop her fall. Her body followed and her hip plowed into the metal support with a painful *thwack.* A movement from below, through the open space between two stairs, caught her attention, but she was wincing and it was dark and all she saw was a woman's form in silhouette retreating.

And then Luke was all over her.

"Are you all right?" At her side, he scooped one arm around her waist to right her. "What the hell happened?"

"I'm not sure."

A few other people who'd seen her almost fall gathered round to make certain she was okay.

"You need to make out a report," a young woman said. "Obviously these stairs are dangerous."

Helen was looking down now, to see what her heel could possibly have caught on. Damned if she could tell.

"Want me to call the club manager?" a lawyer type asked.

"No, really."

"You're sure?" Luke asked, slipping an arm around her waist and providing support.

"I'm fine."

But as she started up the stairs, she realized her sandal wasn't fine. She stopped to remove it.

"What's with the shoe?"

The dainty sandal was ruined, Helen realized. "The heel—it's broken."

It was, in fact, half-hanging off the sole.

"You must have caught it on the edge of the step," Luke mused.

"Maybe."

That might explain what happened.

Either that, or someone below the stairs had

grabbed onto the heel and torqued it hard enough that it gave under her weight.

Disturbed by the thought, Helen wondered if she should say something. But what? That maybe someone had purposely tried to make her fall?

Who?

And why?

Having barely gotten a glimpse of the shadow moving below the stairs, she couldn't describe her supposed attacker. If she had, indeed, been attacked. The incident had been so subtle, she simply wasn't sure.

And so when they arrived back at the table and Annie frowned up at the sandal in Helen's hand, then asked what happened, Helen said, "I had a case of clumsy."

"That's what you get for wearing these ridiculous pieces of…well, whatever it is," Nick said, taking the sandal from her hand. "Let me go see if I can work some magic."

"You think you can find a shoemaker at this time of night?" Luke asked.

"No, but I have connections here." Nick slid away, sandal and Isabel in tow.

"Connections?" Luke echoed.

"Name's Gideon," Helen told him. "The owner. Although I've never heard that shoe repair was one of his specialties." She sighed. "And those were my favorites."

"Who cares about a shoe," Luke said.

"Sacrilege," Annie warned him.

"I care about *the woman.*"

The statement made Helen feel warm inside. ''I'm all right, really.''

''But if you hadn't caught yourself, you could have broken something.''

''Well, nothing is broken or even sprained,'' she assured him. ''I might be a little stiff in the morning and have a bruise or two, but—''

''Bruise where?''

''My hip rammed that railing.''

Luke said, ''Maybe we should get you to a doctor.''

''Not necessary. Really.''

Helen was touched by Luke's worry, and certainly she would seek medical attention if she were hurt. Thankfully, he didn't press the issue, merely sat close, arm around her back, and lent his silent support.

''So what do you think about Nick's video?'' Annie asked. ''Was that really simply a declaration of love…or a proposal?''

''Proposal?'' Helen echoed.

The thought stunned her. Nick in a relationship was difficult enough to fathom. But Nick married?

''C'mon, you have to know he's serious about Isabel. And Nick says things best with his camera.''

''Maybe.''

Maybe both of her friends would be getting married soon—that was sure to change the dynamics between them. It would be great for her friends, of course. Not so great for her. She depended on them being there to cheer her on, listen to her gripes and keep her honest.

Helen tried to force away any negativity. She shifted in her seat, then was hard-pressed not to grunt in discomfort lest she worry Luke. If she was this sore now, what would she feel like in the morning? Thank God, she'd had her wits about her or she *might* have broken something.

Which prompted her to rethink the incident more closely. The thought that it might not have been an accident nagged at her.

"You know," she said suddenly, "I'm not really sure what happened on the stairs."

Annie frowned. "I thought you said you got clumsy."

"Yeah, maybe."

"You're not sure?" Nate asked.

Now *he* looked worried, as well. And Helen felt Luke's arm tense against her back.

"My heel caught somehow, but when I looked to see on what...nothing."

Annie said, "It is pretty dark on those stairs."

"It is," Helen agreed.

Luke gave her an intent look. "I hear a but."

"I'm probably imagining it."

"What?"

"That someone grabbed hold of the heel of my sandal. I mean, it kind of felt like that. And then afterward, when I looked through the opening between stairs, a woman was moving away pretty fast."

"What woman?" Luke asked. "What did she look like?"

"Got me. If you think it's dark on the stairs, it's even darker beneath them."

"You think someone simply had too much to drink and was playing a prank on you?" Annie asked, sounding hopeful.

"That must be it, right?"

"All right, what am I missing here?" Luke asked.

"Our ladies are being extra paranoid," Nate told him. "Just because Annie had a stalker—"

"Stalker?"

"I don't think I have a stalker," Helen protested. "This is an isolated incident."

"If you don't count the things that have been happening at the café," Annie countered.

"What things?" Luke gazed at Annie intently. "You mean the espresso machine breaking down?"

She nodded. "And right before that someone left lines of white powder in the rest room—talcum powder that looked like cocaine. And then there was the spoiled food and the electrical problem."

"Now you think someone caused the electrical problem?" Nate asked.

"Well, it's possible," Helen said, wondering if her friend could be on to something.

"And it's possible your paranoia has hit a new high, Helen."

At which point her friend turned on her fiancé. "Nate!"

"Well, come on, Annie!"

Helen grimaced. "Please, stop. Don't argue on my account." Bad enough that her supposed accident had spoiled Nick and Isabel's big night. She didn't want hurt feelings between Annie and Nate, as well. "I'm sorry I brought it up."

Luke leaned in and nuzzled her hair, then whispered in her ear. "We should talk about this later."

Helen didn't argue, though she had other things in mind for later. If she could move, that was. Her back was starting to stiffen.

Nick and Isabel returned, followed by the dark-haired owner, whose deep blue eyes were filled with concern.

"What can I do to make you feel better?" Gideon asked, returning her footwear with a flourish.

"I'm fine," she assured him. "And you already did it. You fixed my sandal."

"Super glue. It should do long enough to get you home, but be careful walking. Don't take any chances. Let a professional fix it properly. Better yet, buy yourself a new pair on me. Don't spare the expense."

"That's not necessary."

"All right. Then call it a whim. Indulge me."

Realizing that if she objected she would be making a big deal over a nice gesture, Helen shrugged. "All right."

Everyone at the table clapped, except for Luke who squeezed her shoulder. Helen tried not to wince. Another sore spot. How many would she have?

Gideon ordered the table another bottle of champagne on the house, then took his leave.

Helen tried to clear her mind of the accident on the

stairs, but the confusing thoughts lingered and, for her, the evening was tainted.

Some second date.

HELEN HAD GROWN unusually quiet after the discussion about her continuing bad luck. Having known none of this but for the espresso-maker problem, Luke now was seriously troubled. Was Helen simply having a string of bad luck, as Nate had suggested, or was something else going on?

Was this a repeat of the things that happened to those other competitors who had gone out of business after a Hot Zone moved into their territory?

While the thought had occurred to him before, he'd always put their failures to bad business or bad luck. He'd never seen their points of view from the inside. He'd never been connected to another owner as he was to Helen.

He'd had nothing to do with her bad luck, not personally. But what if…

When Helen set her champagne glass on the table, Luke noted she winced. Knowing she wouldn't agree to an emergency room visit—and truth be told, it really did seem unnecessary—Luke had an alternate idea.

"Hey, darlin', you look a little tired," he murmured, his lips in her hair.

"It's been a long day."

"Just say the word."

"The word," she echoed softly. Then louder, she

said to her friends, ''I think we're going to get going.''

''Already?'' Annie asked. Then her eyebrows shot up knowingly. ''Have fun with the rest of your evening.''

''Don't do anything I wouldn't do,'' Nick said with a wicked grin.

''I would need another set of morals to compete with what you wouldn't do,'' Helen jibed.

The friends all hugged and kissed and then he and Helen were out of there.

As they exited the club, Luke thought he certainly would like to take Annie's advice and have some fun—he'd been counting on it earlier—but his first concern was for Helen. Her spine appeared stiff and she was walking a little too carefully.

He flagged down a taxi, got Helen settled inside, then gave the driver the address.

''You're taking me to Hot Zone?'' she asked.

''For a completely therapeutic reason. The hot tub checked out A-okay this morning. A good soaking will loosen you up a lot.''

''Hmm. In what way?'' she asked softly.

Luke couldn't help his perfectly natural reaction to her suggestive question. ''You decide,'' he murmured, running his hand down her arm.

She shuddered slightly under his touch, and his response was so intense that Luke thought he might go out of his mind with wanting her.

He'd never wanted anyone more. Chances were, he never would.

She cleared her throat, moved closer, and in a low voice said, "I, uh, don't have a swimsuit on me."

"No problem," he said, his lips once more in her hair. "You are wearing underwear, right?"

For a moment he thought that maybe she wasn't, for she didn't immediately respond.

Then she cleared her throat again and murmured, "Um, uh-huh," in a way that made the small hairs on his arms stand up at attention.

Must be some underwear!

The thought made him shift in his seat. He couldn't wait to see why Helen was so uncomfortable about her undergarments. Then as the taxi pulled over to the curb, Luke remembered the type of shop her best friend owned. Heat flushed through him, and his imagination was already engaged as he handed the cabbie a bill and waved away the change.

He helped Helen out of the taxi and guided her to the front door where he fumbled with the keys, all the while trying to keep that imagination in check. Once inside, he turned on only enough lights so they could walk across the main floor of the café to the hot tub in safety.

For the first time, he thought the building had too many windows and too much light.

If Helen was going to strip, he didn't want anyone seeing her exotic lingerie—or anything else—but him.

10

HELEN CHECKED HERSELF OVER in the mirrored wall and fought her nerves. The peach-colored bra was of a thin material, but everything that mattered was covered. The matching panties were a high-thigh cut and rose to her waist, nearly covering the bruise starting to bloom on her hip, a reminder of the accident. *If* it had been an accident…

Other than the sensual color, the lingerie seemed fairly conservative and showed no more flesh than did her two-piece bathing suit.

At least not yet, it didn't.

She'd looked forward to Luke peeling off her clothing and discovering the lovely undergarments, had anticipated his pleasure when the mood-altered material did its magic. But waltzing out to the hot tub next-to-nude for Luke's inspection was somehow intimidating.

Helen flushed with anticipatory heat. Then, giving herself a last glance in the mirror, she started—was it her imagination, or had the peach tone faded slightly? She grew even hotter.

What would happen to the material when it got wet?

Wrapping a luxurious bath towel around her, Helen decided it was time to find out.

Luke was already in the hot tub, which was big enough for a dozen people. Immersed to his chest, he rested his back against the wall of the tub opposite the entry as she approached. She stopped at the edge of the hot tub and—feeling something like an exotic dancer in a gentleman's club—removed the towel and let it puddle to the floor.

His eyes were on her every movement. He didn't hide his thoughts, that was for certain. As his gaze flicked over her, his handsome features grew taut with hunger.

But somehow his voice managed to sound perfectly normal when he asked, "Do you need help getting in?"

"Stay where you are!" She gripped the handrail on each side and carefully stepped down a level so that hot water swirled around her calves. "I—I mean, no thanks. I'm fine."

"You certainly are."

Sinking down to her chin in the hot, bubbly water not only felt fabulous but gave Helen a sense of temporary relief. She could hide from Luke, at least until they got out...*if* she chose to hide.

"Better?" he asked.

"Oh, yeah."

"Get right up to one of the jets. That'll loosen up your back in no time."

Helen did as he suggested, and as the water began pounding her stiff spine, she breathed deeply. Eyes closed, she dropped her head forward and luxuriated in the water pulsing up and down her spine.

For a few moments, she let magic happen.

Even so, the reason for her discomfort kept plaguing her. What if her tripping on the stairs hadn't been an accident? What if Annie had been right?

Was someone out to get her—both professionally or personally?

Not wanting to dwell on the negative at the moment, she opened her eyes slightly and gazed at Luke through her lashes. He was still focused on her.

"Luke...why do I have the feeling you had a hot tub excursion in mind for tonight no matter what?"

"Because you have a naturally suspicious nature."

"I think that's one of my most endearing qualities."

Not that her friends would necessarily agree.

"I can think of a few even better ones," Luke said, moving to the jet next to hers.

His presence was a tangible thing, and even though he wasn't touching her, she imagined he was—in her fertile mind the whirling waters becoming his fingers. Suddenly she wondered if he was wearing underwear, as well, or if he kept a bathing suit around.

Then, again, he could be wearing nothing at all.

Though she wanted in the worst way to look down through the water to check for herself, she kept her eyes on his face and sighed again.

"Good?" he asked.

"Wonderful."

"I could make it even better," he said, moving closer until he was before her, right in her face.

Only his eyes weren't on her face. They were aimed lower, and his expression was open, revealing his surprise.

"Something wrong?" she asked, taking a quick look down and finding out exactly what happened when her mood underwear got hot. She guessed it didn't matter if lust or hot water heated it up, the material simply reacted.

"Your underwear—it seems to have..." he cleared his throat, "...disappeared."

And he seemed to be staring at her nipples; the blush of her full areolas was fully revealed through the transparency, she realized.

Her immediate reaction was to sink lower.

"So is it supposed to do that? Disappear? Or is it the water?"

"Uh-huh."

His eyebrows raised and his voice grew throaty. "I'll take that as a yes on both counts."

And he moved even closer so that she suddenly grew unbearably warm. She wondered if, with all this heat, her lingerie might possibly melt right off her.

Helen swallowed hard as Luke moved right into her personal space. His leg bobbed against hers, and he was doing something incredibly erotic to her shin with his foot.

"Feeling looser?" he murmured, the low timbre of his voice making her quake inside.

Helen thought she could take his question two ways. ''Much.'' Let him figure out what she meant.

''So you're ready for anything?''

''Not quite anything...''

''Within the parameters of a second date,'' he qualified, moving so that he was in front of her.

''We'll see.''

''When?''

''The date's not ended yet.''

''I thought you only had that one rule.''

He settled in closer so that if she moved, her breasts would brush against his chest. She wanted to...but fought the urge...taking pleasure in drawing out the anticipation.

''Right.''

''I don't remember timing being part of it. Unless you left out a clause.''

Her forehead furrowed with her puzzlement. ''Huh?''

He surrounded her with himself, placing his hands on the edge of the hot tub rim on either side of her. Somehow, he kept from touching her.

''Do we have to wait until the end of the date to kiss?'' he murmured.

''Well, no, b—''

Her *but* was swallowed by his mouth covering hers. Any objection floated away on a bubble of instant euphoria. His kiss was long and slow and as wet as the water lapping over them. She could drown in his kisses, Helen thought hazily, not wanting the feeling to end.

But all too soon his mouth released hers only to dip lower. He nibbled along the line of her jaw…drank from the length of her throat…sucked at the softness of a nipple.

The sensitive tip hardened and elongated as he rolled it with his tongue and then bit down lightly with his teeth. She threaded her fingers through his hair and pulled his head back up and kissed him with more passion than she'd ever felt for any man.

Wanting him…knowing it wasn't yet time…knowing that the time would soon be at hand and then they would be through…was killing her.

When he pulled away, she wanted to protest, but he scooped his hands down under her tush and lifted her. She shoved her hands against the tub rim behind her for balance.

"What are you doing?"

"Relax. That's the point here, isn't it?"

Her limbs felt like rubber, but inside she was coiled as tightly as a spring. And as his hands smoothed her flesh, her skin felt equally tight. He spread her thighs and kissed his way down her belly. Then he pulled back slightly, stopping a moment, and she realized he was staring at her. She knew he could see everything through the transparent panties.

Ever so slowly, he caught the delicate material with his teeth…nuzzled her…then dipped his head lower between her thighs.

The water lapped over his face and into her as he parted her with his tongue. Sensation swamped her, and she cried out. Her back bowed and her head went light. But as if sensing she was about to come—and apparently determined to deny her that pleasure just yet—he pulled away and turned her in his arms.

Her breath heaved in her chest.

He smiled a wicked smile.

She arched and pressed her lower body into him. And her question was answered.

No underwear.

No swimsuit.

Only him.

"No fair," she breathed as she surrounded him with her legs and pulled him closer.

The hard length of him pressed into her softness, and as he kissed her again, he began rocking against her. She moaned into his mouth. He slid hands under her and tilted her so that she opened for him and the tip of his cock pushed at her through the material.

She wanted to protest.

She couldn't say a word.

Her world was spinning and she didn't want it to stop. She'd been so close to coming...she couldn't go through that again.

But determined that she wouldn't come alone, she slid a hand between their bellies and found him ready. She played him with her fingertips and bit him with her nails. His groan made her hotter. More wicked. She encircled him and thrust the circle of her fingers down his length.

"Helen," he murmured, biting her neck. "I want you. Need you."

As she wanted and needed him. Now. She couldn't wait for another date. She simply didn't have the will.

"Then take me!" she urged him.

She wouldn't think about it. If she thought about it, she might change her mind. Instead, she flicked the delicate crotch of her panties to the side and guided his tip to her entrance, taking him from the warmth of the hot tub to the heat inside her. He gave a triumphant grunt as he buried himself in her.

She let go of him and lay back in the water, wedged her hands against the sides of the hot tub, allowed him greater penetration.

He swore softly, the sound sheer pleasure, as he slowly pulled back, so that just his tip remained in her before he slid in to the hilt.

His hands were on her breasts now. Kneading them. Rolling her nipples through the thin material between his fingers and thumbs. And then his hands scooped under her tush and balanced her against him.

"Let go," he whispered. "I have you. Trust me."

Trusting that he would make her feel good, that he would make love to her like no other man ever had, she let go.

"Now touch yourself, Helen. I want to watch."

Feeling like it was the most natural thing in the world, she cupped her breasts and visually teased him as he so obviously wanted. His lids heavy with desire, through half-closed eyes he watched her flick her nipples and bite her lips as sensation spiraled down from her breasts to her center.

"That's it. Lower."

Heat searing every inch of her, feeling as if she were in a wet dream, Helen slid a hand down her stomach and inside her panties. The tip of her finger met the sex-swollen nub and rolled over it. A small cry escaped her. She clenched him inside her, held him tight, and then released. Squeezing her buttocks, she rocked against him.

"More," he urged, licking his lips as if he were dry inside. "Faster."

She responded and he increased his tempo too and suddenly she felt herself slipping…slipping…

"Now!" she cried, but he stopped her before the quake inside her had a chance to take hold.

"Trust me."

She heard his words through a haze as he pulled out of her and turned her around and bent her at the waist. Then he was inside her again, from behind. He lifted her thighs, opening her to the power of the lower jet.

The fiercely bubbling water caught her so that she couldn't speak. And when she didn't object, he moved her in even closer to the rushing underwater spray.

"Your nipples," he murmured into her hair as he began to rock against her. "Pluck them. I want to watch you make them hard."

Closing her eyes, she did as he asked. He inched forward, dropping her to her knees on the submerged bench, closer to the jet that increased the rhythmic pressure on her clit. Her eyes flew open, and feeling as though she might split in two from the pleasure, she cried out.

"I—I can't..."

"Yes," he insisted, rolling them both forward. "Let me watch."

The jet caught her just right and forced her limpid arms to move, her boneless fingers to tug at her nipples, while he slid in and out of her like he would never stop.

She didn't want him to...she wanted the impossible...for this to go on forever.

But then he bit the soft spot between her neck and shoulder and she couldn't stop herself from careening over the edge. Wave over wave of hot pleasure poured out of her until she felt boneless.

Luke shuddered behind her and held her tight against him, guiding her away from the jet.

Shaking and weak, she was content to rest against him as he smoothed her body with his hands and kissed her neck and shoulders. When his hands found her breasts through the transparent material and exactly copied what she had done to them, she felt stirrings of renewed desire. Smiling, knowing it was far too soon to do anything about it, she sighed and luxuriated in the lazy pleasure.

But then he moved her closer to the side again, his hands sliding down her body to the inside of her thighs, his fingers moving aside the panties and disappearing deep inside her. His thumb flicked her clit, and before she could respond, the pressure built once more.

"No, not without you," she protested, but he had her pinned, her back to his front, and she was torn about what she did and didn't want, so allowed him to do what he would.

He proceeded to make her come. Once. Twice.

Then he was in her…filling her…making her want…making her need.

And when he took her home what seemed like hours later and she thought they were both spent and couldn't possibly take more, he proved her wrong in the down comfort of her own bed.

It was only in the small, still hours before morning was yet defined that she lay awake in the dark, listening to his light snore, staring at the ceiling and thinking about what she'd really done.

She'd cheated.

She'd defied her own rule.

She'd skipped the second date limit and gone straight to the third.

Now what?

FOR ONCE Luke awoke without a hard-on. He registered the fact even as he registered the lush room that reminded him of Helen. Not that she was anywhere to be seen.

But his memory of her was so vivid. Her scent lingered on the sheets, all mixed with the musk smell of their mating. He took a deep whiff and felt stirrings in his lower regions. He wasn't spent, after all.

Smiling, he lay back and replayed snatches of the night before in his mind, so that when Helen returned to the bedroom, two mugs in hand, his interest was obvious.

"I thought you could use an eye-opener."

"They're open. And I'm up."

"So I see."

But she was avoiding looking at his erection. She handed him one mug, then moved to the mirrored dresser where she used her free hand to finger-comb her hair. Sipping at the coffee laced with chicory—now how had she guessed that was one of his favorites?—Luke watched her every move.

Her satin dressing gown slid sensuously over her full curves, and Luke couldn't stay glued to the bed when what he wanted was to take her in his arms and make love to her again. He set down his mug and came up behind her. Meeting her gaze in the mirror, he dipped his head to kiss the side of her neck.

For a moment, she acquiesced, allowed him free access to the delicious flesh. Then, as if thinking better of it, she pulled away and turned to face him.

"Work," Helen murmured, placing a hand flat against his chest.

"We have time."

Luke moved closer so that she was trapped between him and the dresser, but that hand stayed put between them. Tension wired from her, but not the tension of mutual attraction. Helen wanted him on some level—Luke knew that. But she was wary, and he figured seducing her wouldn't be a piece of cake this morning.

Was she regretting last night? he wondered, remembering how they'd broken her rules again and again.

Wanting her more than ever, he murmured, "Don't I get a good morning kiss?" as he slid his hands around her waist and settled them on her hips.

She winced in response and he immediately let go.

"Helen?"

"The hip. I banged it, remember? That was the reason we got in that hot tub in the first place."

Maybe the reason she'd forgotten her damn rules. She'd felt vulnerable. And he'd taken advantage of that, even if not consciously.

Fighting guilt, Luke backed off. "Have you thought any more about who would want to hurt you?"

She shook her head. "I was thinking maybe *you* could tell me."

"Me?" He narrowed his gaze at her. "You think *I* had something to do with your getting hurt?"

"Well, you said we should talk about it later. This is later. And no, not directly, no."

"Indirectly, then."

"Bad things keep happening to your competitors."

He swore under his breath and turned away from her, spotting his briefs across the room where Helen had tossed them in a moment of passion. No passion in her now, Luke thought, climbing into them, then gathering his clothing and throwing it on the rumpled bed.

"Are we back to square one?" He started to dress. "Have I given you any reason to distrust me?"

"I never said that. And I told you I saw a woman under the stairs at the club."

"But you're acting like I should know something...or is that simply your excuse for the day?"

"Excuse?"

He started dressing. "A reason for not sleeping with me. Even though you've wanted me from the moment we met, you always seem to need an excuse, last night being the unexpected exception."

"Last night was a mistake," she said, voice tight. "We don't even know each other."

"As if we would know each other way better if we waited for one more final date. I know enough about you to think you're someone I can care for, Helen. The problem is, you won't let me get close enough to find out for sure. Those damn rules of yours are enough to put off any man."

"Well, good, then my diabolical plan is working."

He started at her sarcastic tone, and at her physically defensive body language, one arm wrapped around her middle, the other hand at her throat.

Was that her problem? That she thought he meant to hurt her, and if she couldn't prove that he'd done so physically, she would convince herself of his bad emotional intentions and use that against him?

It was all too much for him to take in right now. He had tomorrow's opening to worry over, and—checking his Rolex—less than thirty hours to go. Besides, he'd never been good at the relationship thing. What in the world had made him think he would know how to do it right with Helen?

"You're right. Work is waiting," he said.

Luke hesitated a moment, just to see if Helen would whisper a soft word, perhaps offer a goodbye kiss. But she stood there, looking victimized, and he didn't know what he could do other than leave.

Wondering if that was it—if Helen would use the excuse that they'd already had sex as a reason not to see him—he took off and jogged the few blocks to Hot Zone.

The first person he ran into was Flash, sipping at a coffee from a Helen's Cybercafé cup.

One look at him and she lowered the cup and her eyebrows shot right up into her red hair. "Couldn't stop at home to change first?" the publicity director asked. "You and your date must have had some night."

With that, she swept by, leaving him with an odd feeling.

How did Flash know what he'd been wearing the night before...*unless she'd been at the club.*

11

HELEN WENT OVER Luke's accusations a multitude of times as she walked to the café later.

Thankfully, Kate had opened for her this morning. She'd called to make certain her assistant had things under control, then had tried to get herself together. For the first time since starting the business, she was late and couldn't even work up enough guilt to care.

What was wrong with her?

Luke. Every time she closed her eyes for a moment, she saw his face. Dark eyes...broad forehead...high cheekbones...and that incredibly sexy dimple.

It wasn't supposed to be like this.

She wasn't supposed to be hurting.

She was the one who was supposed to do the leaving—and after three dates, not two—but it had been he who'd left her.

She wasn't finished with him yet for more than one reason. Thinking that his assistant was romantically attracted to Luke, she'd meant to question him about Alexis Stark.

About the depth of their relationship.

About whether or not he thought the young woman

might be capable of illegally driving his competitors out of business in his behalf.

About whether or not Alexis could have been jealous enough to hurt her romantic competition the night before.

But Luke had made it personal in a different way, ragging on her about not wanting to sleep with him or get close to him because she didn't trust him.

Did she?

With her business, yes...but with her heart?

Luke had said he could care about her, but that she was keeping him from finding out for sure. Her and her damn rules, huh? He simply didn't understand and she doubted he would try to, which was just as well.

Right?

Torn, Helen approached the cybercafé, which was busy but not insanely so. Weekends had more traffic in general throughout the day without the hugely busy morning rush.

Entering the storefront, she looked around. Only three people at the counter, but half the seating was taken. A few of the regulars were there—Tilda over by the windows, Sam at his preferred computer, Annie at their usual table. Her best friend grinned and waved her over.

Helen stopped to check with Kate, who was being helped by one of the college kids. "Everything going all right?"

"Yeah, fine."

Kate didn't exactly sound fine, but she was working as if nothing was wrong. Now feeling a little guilty—Helen knew she'd probably been relying on her new assistant manager too much lately to take over for her—she nevertheless chose to join Annie for a few minutes. She slid into the chair across from her friend.

One look at her face and Annie frowned. "Okay, what's wrong?"

"What do you think?"

No use in avoiding the issue. She couldn't lie to her friends, and Annie would pry the truth out of her if she had to use pliers.

"I'm not a mind reader, Helen. You need to be a little more explicit. What happened last night after you left Club Undercover?"

"The dirty deed happened."

Behind her lenses, Annie's eyes went round. "Yikes! Congratulations!"

"Save it."

"I don't think so. You *never* break your own rules and this is the second time—well, that I know of. And this is the big one. Luke DeVries has got to be something special."

"He's something, all right. He's gone."

Helen gave Annie the two-minute version of what had gone down between them that morning.

Annie patted her hand. "So you had words. It happens in the best of relationships."

Relationships?

The word nearly choked Helen, but somehow she spit out, "He left."

"He had work to do."

Helen shook her head.

But rarely one to see the dark side of life, Annie said, "Luke's doesn't strike me as the kind of man who gives up on things he really wants."

"What makes you think he wants me?"

"Despite the specs, I'm not blind. Wow, Nick was right. You did really take a tumble."

"I never said any such thing."

"C'mon, admit it."

"It's simply that I like to be in charge when it comes to calling it quits," Helen hedged, not in the mood to examine any more truths for one day.

"And you usually pick guys who are good with that. They go with your flow. Luke has other ideas. He just might be the right man for you."

"You think I need a man to control me?"

"I think you need a man in your life who is as strong as you are," Annie told her. "Who else can deal with you? It's time you stopped avoiding the possibility of having a real relationship."

"Look who's talking. At least I never stopped dating."

"Let's not point fingers. I had my problems," Annie admitted. "But I got over it and now I have Nate. And you could have Luke if you put your mind to it."

"You know I'm not interested in anything permanent."

"Uh-huh."

"And don't patronize me."

"No, ma'am."

If she didn't know Annie loved her and wanted to see her happy, Helen might have been tempted to strangle the smaller woman.

A sudden flurry of sound and movement from the corner of her eye caught her attention. Sitting in one of the upholstered chairs, a young woman was swatting at her legs.

Helen rose and moved to investigate. "Excuse me, but is something wrong?"

"Something's biting me," the young woman complained.

She continued to brush at her legs and people started to stare.

"Hey, something's biting me, too." This from the woman on the couch, who was scratching her ankle. "Jeez, I think there are fleas in this place."

A murmur rippled through the café, but before Helen could protest that of course her café didn't have fleas, she saw a tiny dark fleck jump from the woman's leg and out of sight. Horrified, she clenched her jaw so she wouldn't gape.

"It's her." The woman's male companion was pointing at Tilda. "Look at the dirty old hag—she brought fleas into the place."

"I didn't do nothin' wrong," Tilda protested, looking freaked by the accusation.

"No, of course not," Helen said. Or at least not on purpose.

"My clothes are clean," Tilda went on.

"Yeah, just look at 'em," the guy returned sarcastically.

Helen said, "Excuse me, sir, but please refrain from—"

He jumped to his feet. "I have eyes." And to the woman he was with, he said, "Let's get out of here."

"Gladly."

They scurried out of the place, followed by half her customers, including Tilda. Those remaining appeared torn. And then a guy started scratching his legs.

"I think I'd better call an exterminator," Helen said, "but I want to make this up to all of you, so on your way out, stop at the counter and Kate will give you a coupon for a free drink of your choice next time you stop by."

An invitation that didn't have to be offered twice. But not all the remaining customers bothered to get that coupon. And to her horror, Helen heard more than one person say they wouldn't be back, that if they wanted coffee, they would go over to Hot Zone from now on.

"Oh, boy," Annie said. "What now?"

"Now I get an exterminator."

Suspicions aroused, she thought Tilda got a bad rap. The homeless woman being responsible for the sudden infestation, when she'd never caused any such problem before, was simply too convenient. Too convenient that this highly effective way of driving out customers happened just when Hot Zone was about to open. For the moment, however, she kept that speculation to herself.

"I can leave the shop to Gloria if you need help," Annie offered.

"Thanks, but I think we'll have to clear out of here, too, as soon as I can."

"When you do, come on over."

Annie gave her a hug and headed for the door.

"Kate, would you lock up behind Annie and put the Closed sign in the front window?"

"Anything you say."

"Then clean up and take the rest of the day off. With pay."

Helen was already sitting down to a computer, where she brought up Yellow Pages. Within minutes, she was on the telephone trying to get one of the local exterminating services to see to her situation today, weekend emergencies always being a nightmare for a business.

But by the time Kate had cleaned up, she'd found someone who promised to be there within the hour.

"What about tomorrow?" Kate asked.

"Plan on working, although it depends on what the exterminator says about how long it will take. I'll let you know if we can't open first thing for some reason."

"What a time to have this happen," Kate said with a sigh. "If we can't open tomorrow...well, that means Hot Zone will get our business."

Kate's parting observation put a knot in Helen's stomach. She was correct, of course. Who knew how many customers she would lose over this?

"Kate, wait a minute," she said, catching her assistant at the door. ''You know Luke's public relations director, right? Tall woman, red hair.''

''Big mouth? Yeah, I know who she is.''

''Did she by any chance stop by this morning?''

''Bright and early,'' Kate said. ''Both she and the other one. Short with dark hair. What's her name?''

''Alexis.'' Who'd been in and out of the place quite a bit lately, Helen thought, quickly adding things up in her mind. ''The two of them were here together?''

''Cozy as you please right over there on that couch. Too bad the fleas didn't get them, huh?''

With that, Kate exited.

Leaving Helen staring at the flea-ridden couch and wondering if Alexis Stark was doing a whole lot more than worshiping Luke DeVries from afar.

HELEN STOPPED BY Annie's Attic later to catch her friend up on the bad news.

''You're shut down until Monday?''

''At least.'' A sick feeling passed through Helen as she remembered the edict. ''And I just wonder who called a city health inspector.''

''You had a couple of highly unhappy customers,'' Annie said.

''Or a highly competitive—and jealous—woman, who decided to close me down so everyone who wanted coffee would check out Hot Zone during its grand opening.''

She quickly shared her suspicions concerning Alexis.

''You think she would go as far as to try to hurt you personally?''

''I think she's in love with Luke. And if she's done what I think...''

''I get your point.''

''You know my cousin Julio could take on this problem for you,'' Gloria Delgado said, pausing as she unpacked new product to make the offer.

Annie's assistant manager looked so outraged for her that Helen actually bit back a smile. Good-hearted Gloria wanted to solve all the problems in her corner of the world, but her methods were a little...well, primitive.

''Thanks, Gloria, but I think you'll have to keep Julio as your secret weapon awhile longer.''

Gloria rolled her eyes as the front door opened and a customer walked in. ''Nobody listens to me, so I'll go take care of business.''

''Thanks, Gloria,'' Annie said. ''Maybe we should go into the office,'' she suggested to Helen.

''Great.''

Then at least she could sit down and take it all in. Helen felt as if the stuffing were knocked out of her. Problem after problem and now this.

''When did Luke's competitors start having such bad luck?'' Annie asked. ''And how long has she worked for him?''

''I don't know.''

''But there's someone who does.''

''I'm not calling Luke, so forget it.''

''Someone has to make the first move.''

"No, actually, no one does."

Luke hadn't called *her,* after all. She'd forgotten her cell phone, but she'd checked her messages on her home phone. Besides, she told herself, you could look at it as they'd already had three dates. Look what an emotional mess she was now. Another shot at it and who knew what might happen?

No, it was better this way.

"You always were too stubborn for your own good. Without his help, how are you going to get the information you need?"

"How do you think?"

Annie raised her eyebrows. "I suppose you want to use my computer."

"That would be helpful since I can't go back into the café—though I could go home."

"Help yourself."

A grateful Helen jumped at the chance to stick around and share with Annie. Going home at this hour of the day would be too dismal. She'd never been crazy about having an abundance of alone time.

A thought that brought her back to Luke, to how much it had hurt when he'd walked out on her.

But not wanting to dwell on the foreign emotion, she forced herself to get to work and focus on finding an answer to the question uppermost in her mind. Did Alexis Stark have it in for her?

A couple of hours later, Helen had exhausted many avenues of Internet research and still wasn't done. Annie came back into the office and perched on the edge of the desk just as Helen was following a new set of links about the Cooper Coffee Company Luke had worked for.

"Well, Sherlock?"

"I've done searches in every town that has a Hot Zone. As far as I can tell, Flash has been with him since he opened his second venue. I'm not sure about Alexis, since she's more low key. But as far as I can tell, she's been around from the beginning, also."

Helen pushed a printout of a photo taken of the crowd at Luke's Phoenix Hot Zone opening two years before. While Luke was in the foreground with a local celebrity, Alexis was there, right behind him, the woman behind the man.

Annie checked it out with interest. "And the competitors started closing down when?"

"Right from the beginning, Annie. So Alexis could be responsible."

"Or this Flash," Annie said, pointing to the tallest woman in the crowd.

"I suppose. If she had a motive."

"Hey, fame and fortune are great motivators. Her star is hitched to Luke's."

"Something to consider. But I have the feeling she has so many connections that she could go anywhere she wants as a PR director."

"What if she has a thing for Luke, too?" Annie suggested. "A successful, good-looking guy like him—a lot of women might have the hots for him."

Including her, Helen thought, wishing the nagging feeling would simply go away and leave her alone.

''So what's the next step?'' Annie asked. ''Are you going to tell him?''

''Oh, right. We fight, he leaves, he doesn't call, then I call him to accuse one of the women he employs of trying to do me in.''

''Works for me.''

''I don't think so.''

''You're going to let it go?''

''I don't know what I'm going to do yet. This isn't proof of anything.'' Helen gathered together her printouts and slid them into her purse. ''I'm hanging on to this stuff, though, until I figure it out.'' Taking a look at the LCD screen, she stopped and stared at another photo of several people—employees of Cooper Coffee Company. ''Whoa, what have we here.''

Annie cocked her head and pointed. ''That is Luke, right?''

''A younger version,'' Helen agreed, quickly scanning the article. ''He was fired.''

''What?''

''From Cooper Coffee Company.''

''Why?''

''Something about his questionable business practices, according to some information I found.''

''That doesn't sound good.''

Helen frowned. ''No, it doesn't. I'm not sure I believe it, either.''

As far as she could tell, Luke had too much integrity to do anything underhanded. Or even questionable. Nevertheless, she printed off that copy, as well.

She didn't have a lot of time to think about what

she'd found, though. Annie called in reinforcements, and before Helen could object, she was off to an early dinner and a movie with her two best buds. On a Saturday night, no less. Date night. They'd given up dates with their lovers to rally around her. A fact that gave Helen hope that, no matter that the rest of her life crumbled, she would always have them.

By the time she arrived home, it was nearly ten and her telephone was ringing. She checked the caller ID—Luke—and picked it up anyway.

"Hello." She tried not to sound breathless.

"Where have you been? I've been worried sick about you!"

Luke...worried?

Her pulse ticked faster. "Dinner and a movie with Nick and Annie."

Was that a sigh of relief she heard?

"There was no answer on your cell or at the cybercafé," Luke said. "I tried all afternoon. I swung by and saw the health inspector's notice plastered in the window. What the hell happened?"

"I had to call an exterminator."

"I never saw any roaches—"

"Fleas."

Silence. Then, "I'm not liking this."

"Neither am I."

"I had nothing to do with it."

"I didn't think you did."

"Then why didn't you call me?"

"I didn't think you would be interested."

He cursed softly, then said, "Helen, if you don't know how interested I am by now..."

And Helen found herself breathing a deep sigh of relief. "I mean...you had other things on your mind."

"I would always make time for you."

Helen swallowed hard at the sentiment.

"That's what I was trying to tell you this morning," he went on.

"About this morning..."

"Can we let it go?"

"Sure," she said, confusion flooding her.

"And let me make it up to you in person?"

The thought made her tingle all over. She could only imagine how he would do so.

Still, she asked, "Now? It's late."

"So we'll go to bed."

Nothing sounded better. That was the problem. When it came to Luke DeVries, her control slipped away all too easily.

Determined to take back control and keep it, she said, "Not tonight."

"When, then?"

"I—I don't know." Her stomach was quickly twisting into a knot.

"Tomorrow."

"Tomorrow is your opening."

Luke sounded utterly sincere when he said, "And I can't think of anyone I want there at my side more."

But he was the competition. Could she really do it? With her shop closed under mysterious circumstances, could she really flaunt her...well, whatever Luke and she had...before God and everyone *and* in his arena?

She chose to be honest. "I don't know that I can do it, Luke."

"Please. Your being there would mean a lot to me." He paused for a second and when she still didn't agree, said, "Besides, you do owe me a third date—your rule."

"Yeah, my rule." Like they were still playing by them. She sighed. Her being there would mean a lot to him. No man had ever said that to her before. Part of her wanted to please him, so she said, "I'll think about it."

"Good! I can't pick you up, but the opening runs from three until eight. Come anytime. I'll expect you. Don't disappointment me."

But she wouldn't make any promises and Luke finally stopped pushing.

"See me in your dreams, darlin'," he said in that low velvet tone that made her toes curl. "'Cause I know you'll be in mine."

As if she could sleep.

12

LUKE SEARCHED the surging Hot Zone crowd for any sign of Helen—*again*—but the effort was in vain.

"Hot damn, boss, we did it," Alexis said. "We have another success on our hands."

"Seems like."

"Cheer up. It could get worse." She glanced around. "Hmm, the dessert table could use some freshening up. I'll find someone to see to it."

With that, his ever-efficient assistant disappeared into the crowd.

And what a crowd it was.

Not only had the twenty- and thirty-something singles made their expected appearance, but couples of all ages, a few families and even some older folk had been drawn out to see what Hot Zone was all about. Media people were there, too, covering every aspect of the new venue, from the fancy coffees to the hot tub currently occupied by several hired models. He'd thought to make it available to anyone, but reminding him that with a big crowd like this, anything could happen, Alexis had talked him out of it.

What would he do without her?

He didn't want to think about it—didn't want to

believe either of the women working for him could be making Helen's life hell. Not today, of all days. But he knew he would have to face the possibility, and soon.

Curiosity had attracted a steady stream of people from the moment the doors had opened at three until now. Luke checked his watch. Nearly six. He guessed Helen wasn't going to show, after all. He tried to bite back his disappointment, but it filled him with something he could only describe as loss.

How could this be? he wondered, searching the crowd yet again.

There were plenty of beautiful women in the room, including several local celebrities who'd made a point of securing an introduction to him. An actress...a traffic reporter from a local news station...a North Shore debutante who headed a leading charity...he could be wearing any one of them on his arm right this moment.

Trouble was...he didn't want any of them.

He wanted Helen.

Man, was he in trouble!

He couldn't ever remember feeling like this about a woman before. Couldn't ever remember wanting more from a woman than she was willing to give.

He'd lived more than a dozen years of adulthood the same way he had his youth—moving around, having a good time with impermanent relationships, avoiding attachments of any kind. He didn't even have a real place to live, merely a single-bedroom apartment in Houston, the space he occupied on the occasional trip to the Hot Zone corporate office, such as it was. And before opening each new venue, he short-term leased or sublet places in whatever city it was so he had somewhere to keep his things until it was time to move on again.

Suddenly Chicago was looking good to him as a home base.

Great city...even greater Helen.

He could imagine himself traversing every mile of lakefront, exploring every neighborhood, discovering restaurants that no one else knew about...all with her. He could even imagine living in that huge old house of hers, helping her pick out furnishings, digging in the garden and cooking side by side with her in her kitchen.

How had he become such a chump? He was desperate for a woman who didn't even have him on her radar.

Hearing a familiar voice call his name from somewhere across the room—his public relations director was on the prowl—Luke figured he'd better get his butt back in gear. Nevertheless, before going in search of Flash and whichever media mogul she currently had in tow, he gazed around the room one final time.

That's when he spotted her at last.

Practically swallowed by a crowd of her contemporaries, Helen stood out among them. Wearing a low-cut, sleeveless cream-colored dress that clung to her curves as if she'd been poured into it, a gold-toned collar trimmed with green gemstones encircling her neck and thin matching bracelets around her upper arms, her blond hair a riot of curls, she looked for all the world like a goddess.

If only she realized how amazing she was, Luke thought, noting her expression—wary and a little intimidated.

And then her gaze met his and her features immediately softened. Her lips curved into a wide smile and her eyes glittered like emeralds and Luke's stomach did a flip-flop as he shouldered through the crowd to get to her.

He stopped bare inches in front of her, fighting the urge to take her in his arms and kiss her passionately. She would respond…and then be embarrassed to death.

"I didn't think you were going to come," he said.

"I didn't, either."

"What changed your mind?"

"You."

The single word affected him more than he imagined it could. The sound of it turned him on—not a surprise considering they were practically touching—but its intensity kick-started his heart so that he could hear the rush of blood through his ears.

The enormity of his feelings for this woman hit him with the speed and ferocity of a locomotive, but he wouldn't put more specific words to them, not even to himself.

He took her hand and drew it through his arm. "Let me show you around."

"I think I could get around this place in the dark."

They grinned at each other and Luke wished it was

dark, that this shindig was over and he could be alone with her. But, once more, duty called from the across the room.

"Luke, darling!"

Ignoring Flash and leading Helen in the opposite direction, he said, "Then let me show *you* off."

Helen laughed and, sap that he was, Luke now felt as if his heart did a flip-flop.

Physically impossible, he knew, and yet...

With this woman at his side, anything seemed possible.

HELEN HAD TO ADMIT that she was glad she'd taken the plunge to be supportive of Luke. He was returning the favor, quite nicely as a matter of fact. He was keeping her close to his side, as if he meant to protect her, whether from stares in general or from irritating media people, who asked questions that made her feel foolish.

One was stalking her now.

"So you've given up the good fight and have taken the easy way out, have you?" asked a young reporter who wrote for one of the freebies stuffed in business doorways every week.

"I don't understand," she said with a smile both pleasant and forced.

"Your place is under lock and key and you're here, riding the coattails of success."

"Ms. Rhodes is here as my specially invited guest," Luke corrected him, pulling her closer into his side. "If anything, I worship *her*."

"Uh, isn't that a little much?" the guy asked.

"Actually, I thought it somewhat understated," Luke returned. "C'mon, darlin', let's get you some goodies."

Helen barely waited until they were out of the guy's earshot before teasing him. "Goodies... now...in the middle of this circus?"

"What?"

"Goodies...oh, you mean food," she added with mock-innocence.

He raised an eyebrow at her. "Don't tempt me unless you mean it."

Why not? *She* was tempted. She certainly would rather be alone with Luke than in the presence of all these people. But this was his big night and she didn't need to prove anything. No getting around it, she needed to behave herself.

For now.

"Why don't I meet you at the buffet in a few minutes?" she suggested.

"How can I be sure you won't disappear on me?"

"Trust goes two ways, you know." She eyed the line outside the women's locker room. "But don't get anxious if it takes me a while."

Following the direction of her gaze, he said, "You could use the facilities upstairs."

Hating to wait in line for anything, she said, "Great," so he escorted her as far as the stairs, marked off-limits to anyone but employees.

But upon entering the second-floor ladies' lounge,

Helen feared she'd made a mistake. Flash stood before the large mirror and fussed with her hair.

"Helen," she said, voice terse.

"Flash."

Stomach tightening, Helen told herself not to be silly—Alexis was the one who worried her, not Flash—and went about her business.

But when she exited the stall, the public relations director was still there.

As Helen washed her hands, she slid her gaze to the woman who seemed well enough put together that she didn't have to fuss. That umpteenth coat of lipstick Flash was applying had to be her way of stalling for time.

Helen's instincts went on alert.

Part of her wanted to whip back out to the party and the security of having lots of people surrounding her, but another part refused to avoid a potentially uncomfortable situation. That's all it would be, after all. Flash didn't like her.

The feeling was mutual.

And even if it was more than that, even if Flash was the one trying to hurt her business—maybe even trying to hurt *her*—surely she wouldn't try anything with dozens of potential witnesses just below.

Refusing to be cowed, Helen parked herself in front of the mirror, where she finger-combed a few curls back from her face, then reapplied her own lipstick. And all the while, she was aware of the other woman staring at her in the mirror.

"If you have a problem with me, no one is forcing you to stay here," Helen finally said.

She caught a heated look—again indirectly—before the public relations director blinked and masked whatever she'd been thinking.

"What makes you believe I have a problem with you?" Flash asked in her best PR voice.

"You haven't exactly been congenial to your boss's girlfriend."

The word *girlfriend* was out of her mouth before she could stop it and no way was Helen going to give Flash the edge by taking it back.

"Don't get your hopes up where Luke is concerned," Flash said. "You're simply another in a whole lineup of pretty faces Luke amuses himself with when the mood strikes him. In the scheme of things, you're insignificant."

Struck dumb by the direct assault, Helen gaped at Flash before regaining her wits. "What has made you so bitter?" she asked point-blank, unable to help herself. Flash's disregard for her feelings got to her, as did the intimation that Luke was using her. "The fact that you're not one of them?"

Flash laughed. "I'll be with Luke long after you're gone, honey. Which will be sooner than you think. Luke *has* told you about our plans for The Big Apple, hasn't he? As a matter of fact, we have a few Manhattan properties to check out in the next few weeks." Flash's mouth made a red *O*. "Oops, he hasn't told you, has he?"

With a shrug of her shoulders, Flash left Helen to

contemplate an immediate future minus Luke DeVries.

The Big Apple.

He was leaving Chicago for New York City and soon.

What had she expected?

Swallowing the lump in her throat, Helen told herself that it didn't matter. She hadn't expected him to stop expanding his business so that he could stay in Chicago. She hadn't expected anything more than her usual short-lived fling.

Grateful for the reminder of what she had to do to protect herself, Helen thought she ought to thank Flash for straightening her out.

Well…maybe not.

She would simply live in the moment, prepare herself to have the best night of sex ever with Luke before kissing him goodbye for good.

This was their third date, after all.

So why did her dating rule suddenly seem so foolish?

HELEN ALLOWED Luke's positive energy to sweep her along with him as he made the rounds, greeting media types and neighbors with the same panache.

Everyone loved him, she thought.

Everyone…

Closing time drew near and the crowd thinned, and that's when Helen saw Kate, standing at the picked-over dessert buffet alone. Shoving a piece of lemon bar into her mouth, the wraithlike woman peered around until her unhappy gaze connected with Helen's.

And remembering the promise she'd neglected to keep, Helen winced inside.

Since Luke was busy, she slipped away to join her assistant manager. "Hey, I owe you an apology."

"No kidding."

"I'm sorry I forgot to call you this morning. My mind was elsewhere."

Kate's gaze slid over her shoulder where Helen had left Luke. "Yeah, right. Your mind was exactly where it's been for the past week."

"It's been a roller coaster of a week, Kate." Guilt welled in Helen. She'd hired Kate to spell her, but she feared she'd been taking advantage. And now this. "All I can offer you is an apology and a day's pay."

"And you think that's going to buy you my loyalty?"

Uh-oh, that didn't sound good.

Not wanting to lose her first full-time employee—Kate had been a godsend to her—Helen said, "Please tell me you're not going to quit."

"Actually, that's why I'm here." Kate straightened her stance and stuck her chin up in the air. "I thought I might find a job working at Hot Zone."

"Kate, please, no. It's been a bad week. Worse even than you know. I'm pleased with your work and I want you to be happy at the café. I promise things will get better. Don't make up your mind now, not when you're angry with me."

"Well..."

Sensing the young woman was torn, Helen quickly pressed her advantage. "Think about it, okay? Then once we reopen and everything settles down, we'll have time to talk and see if there's something we can work out to make you feel better about your situation."

Kate heaved a sigh. "All right. I'll give you another chance. Assuming you don't forget to call me to tell me the café is open again."

"No more forgetting," Helen said, wondering if it was possible to depend on someone other than herself in business, if not in her intimate life.

Kate left and Helen rejoined Luke, who slipped an arm around her waist and introduced her as his "good friend" to the couple who had his attention.

Good friend...is that what she was?

Better than a poke in the eye, as Nick would say.

Helen tried to shut away any negativity that would affect her last night with Luke, but visions of big red apples danced in her head.

What was happening to her?

Why couldn't she let the conversation with Flash slide and simply enjoy the moment?

Somehow she got through the final hour of the grand opening without Luke catching on. She smiled, she spoke, she supported.

But when the crowd cleared out of Hot Zone and she and Luke were finally alone, she went limp with relief.

Luke was checking things over at the main service

counter, making certain all was to his liking before they could leave. As she watched him attend to small details like the placement of cups and wiping the stainless steel sink dry, Helen felt her throat tighten.

Simply looking at him made her weak in the knees. And in the head. What was happening to her? Helen wondered. How could one man obsess her so?

"Just a few more minutes and we can get out of here," he told her, his voice low and husky with promise.

But rather than being ready for a night of hot sex, Helen needed some straight talk.

She leaned her elbows on the counter and watched his every movement as he peered into the refrigerator and checked over the cartons of milk and half-and-half—things his new employees had already done.

"It must be great to have such loyal employees. What's your secret?"

"I simply treat people who work for me the way I would want to be treated myself." His forehead furrowed as he rounded the counter. "Have you been having *more* problems at your place? Did someone quit?"

"Not exactly. Well, I hope not. My employees all have been transient—part-timers making money while going to school—until I hired Kate." Though Kate had threatened to quit on her, he misunderstood what she was getting at. "Actually, I was wondering about Alexis and Flash."

His "What about them?" wasn't as casual as she

might have expected. She recognized a tension in his voice that immediately put her on edge.

"Do they have any reason to be possessive?"

"Of Hot Zone?"

"Of you."

Luke appeared surprised at that. "Not anything of my doing, if that's what you're asking. I don't consider dating employees ethical. I've always kept my business and personal lives separate. Obviously you have reason to think they feel otherwise."

"Nothing concrete." Not wanting to make accusations she couldn't support, she nevertheless had to bring this out in the open. "Just instinct. Alexis especially. It's the way she looks at you, is so protective of your time, orders the same fancy coffee as you do."

"Right, the coffee," he said, sounding unconvinced. "And Flash?"

There it was again, that tension. Like he knew something about his public relations director he wasn't saying.

Helen shrugged. "I'm not real clear there. But she warned me off you. Basically she told me I was a road stop on your way to The Big Apple."

"New York next was the plan," Luke agreed. "But you're no one's road stop." He thought about it for a moment. "Flash's concern isn't for me personally as much as it is for the business. I never realized how proprietary her interest was until Alexis said something."

"That could be it."

"Jealous?"

He slipped his arms around her and Helen felt something that went beyond sexual attraction.

Pushing the feeling away deep inside her, she said, "Not jealous, worried."

"About?"

"Someone is trying to put me out of business—and before you go there, no, I don't think it's you—but..."

"But you suspect one of my employees."

"Who else is there?"

"I was beginning to wonder myself."

She took a deep breath and touched her forehead to his. "Thank goodness you don't think I'm crazy."

"Well, I didn't say that."

She whipped up her head and met his amused expression. "You're joking, right?"

"Lightening up the mood." He trailed gentle fingers down the side of her face. "I know you're worried. *I'm* worried. I can't say that either Alexis or Flash has done anything overtly suspicious. Still, with all the things that have happened to you, I can't help wondering. And if you were right about someone trying to make you fall on the stairs..."

Luke hugged her close and Helen allowed herself to be comforted for a moment. She couldn't think of any place she would rather be than in his arms. His hand soothing her spine set her nerve endings on edge.

But they weren't done discussing the situation, so she pulled away slightly.

''Alexis or Flash or both seem to be in the wrong place at the right time,'' Helen said. ''Both were in the café right before the coke joke. When my espresso maker was down, Flash walked in and made a fuss. It was as if she *knew* and purposely used the moment to score a big advertisement for Hot Zone.''

''Slamming another business like that is unacceptable.''

''And the couch that was riddled with fleas—they had both been sitting on it earlier, before I got to the café. I can't help believing one of them was responsible for everything. How to prove it, though?''

''I don't know. I'll talk to them both, see if I can get a handle on it, I promise.'' Luke shook his head and sank onto a stool at the counter. ''I didn't want to face this. I didn't want to believe that my success was built on someone purposely making other businesses fail.''

Helen realized the question of culpability really had crossed his mind before. Not that he'd said anything to her—and apparently not to either of the women.

''That's not why you're successful, Luke,'' she assured him. ''It's your ideas and your dedication that have put you where you are. I've watched you work. You're a dynamic personality. You're creative. And your attention to detail—''

''Whoa. I'm convinced.'' He smiled as he pulled her into the vee of his thighs. ''Thank you,'' he murmured, brushing soft lips over hers.

Several somethings stirred in Helen, not only because of the kiss, but because of the bond they'd just forged. Luke believed her and was ready to take action, and she had faith that he would be able to stop the attack on her from continuing.

But another thing had been bothering her. "Luke, when I was doing some research on the history of Hot Zone, I found an article that was odd. About you."

"What about me?"

"Cooper Coffee Company. You were fired... something about your business practices."

His forehead furrowed. "And you want to know why I didn't tell you?"

"Not exactly. I just wanted to know more about it, because it didn't seem...well, like you."

"It wasn't." He sighed and hugged her tight for a moment, then relaxed. "I was trying to get product from a grower in Colombia and the next thing I knew he filed a complaint about me, said I'd threatened to put him out of business if he didn't sign with me."

"I don't believe it."

"My boss did."

"You never figured out what happened?"

"I didn't try," Luke admitted. "I was so angry that I immediately got to work on my business plan for Hot Zone. I was going to show Cooper that I could be a success on my own."

Helen believed him. Odd that he hadn't followed up on the truth of the matter, but she supposed he could have been so disgusted that Cooper believed the grower that he didn't care about keeping his job.

Luke kissed her again and she suddenly wanted

him fiercely. But not here. Not where it was all a game. Afterward, she wanted to lie in his arms, feel his body stretched alongside hers.

When they came up for air, she whispered, "Let's get out of here."

"Your place?"

"Yours."

For, when the night was over, being in his place would make it easier for her to make the break quick and clean.

13

LUKE'S SUBLET was a nice one bedroom with a metal balcony off the living room, but the furnishings were basic, nothing on the walls. Helen guessed that's all a man on the move needed. No attention to detail here, not like in his business. Somehow, she felt the business defined the outer Luke, the one in the media, the one to whom people responded. Surface, she thought. Simply surface. The apartment defined him inside—a loner without roots.

And that fact brought home the rightness of her decision to keep to her rules. It was only a matter of time—soon, Flash had said and he hadn't denied it—before he would be on to The Big Apple and his next conquest.

"Should I make us drinks?" he asked.

"I'm caffeined out."

"Something stronger, then."

"All I want is you." She didn't want to waste one moment of the time they had left together.

"That sounds promising."

He picked up a remote and suddenly the room filled with music that came from every corner. Then he stepped closer, his body tantalizing hers.

"Dance with me," he murmured into her hair.

She didn't hesitate before bringing her body up against his and sliding her hands up to his shoulders. Inching across the floor together was as much a sensual act as it had been at the club. As she'd thought then, they might as well have been having sex.

And why not?

Helen snaked her arms around Luke's neck and kissed him deeply, her emotion a combination of joy and sorrow. Joy that she was safe in his arms and would experience more pleasure than she ever had with another man...sorrow that morning would come all too soon.

He slid his hands down her back to cup her bottom, then pulled her into him so they were truly dancing as one. His erection pressed against her belly and for a while she was content as her flesh warmed. Then wanting more, she lifted a leg and slid it around his thigh, opening herself to his power. Stopping, he groaned in her mouth and hiked her higher, lifting her off the ground completely. Not hesitating, she surrounded him with herself, thighs around his hips, arms around his neck, fingers lost in his hair.

Her body felt like it was melting from the inside out. She kissed his face...his ear...his neck.

Luke groaned and danced her in circles and, in her punch-drunk sexual haze, she realized he was dancing her straight into the bedroom.

Good.

Then they were kissing again and tumbling down onto the unmade bed together.

He flipped her, so her back was against the mattress, and then pulled himself free and got to his feet.

"Where are you going?" she asked.

"Inside you and as soon as possible."

Stripping off his jacket, he threw it on a nearby chair. Faint golden light spilled into the bedroom from the living area and bathed him in a warm glow as he lifted his arms, bringing with them the silk T-shirt he wore. Through slitted eyes, she watched the impromptu strip show and felt her own body respond to every inch he revealed.

Broad shoulders...lean waist...narrow hips...jutting cock.

Her mouth watered at the thought of tasting him.

He slipped off her backless sandals and asked, "How does that dress come off?"

"Peel it," she told him, then watched him work.

He slid the stretchy material up her thighs...over her hips...along her waist. His hands touched every inch of her, testing her patience. Still, she restrained herself from helping him, made the most of the anticipation. She raised her arms over her head even as he reached her breasts.

"Magic underwear?" he breathed, eyeing her exposed flesh.

"Uh-uh. Couldn't wear any under this number without it showing."

Then the dress was magically gone, flipped into the dark, and she was nude and an equally naked Luke was stretched over her, his hands cuffing her wrists up above her head. His erection lay heavy between her thighs. She opened them so he dropped in between, his hot flesh too tempting to ignore. Lifting her hips, she pushed forward, his groan her reward. She rocked against him, created a friction that ignited every nerve inside her.

Opening wider, she rocked again, making her demand obvious.

"No, not yet," he murmured against her mouth.

He drank deeply, stirring her further. Beneath him, her hands still held captive, she brushed his body with her own and felt his erection stir.

He kissed her lips…her cheek…her jaw.

Then, after releasing her hands, he worked his way down her throat…along the valley between her breasts…over her belly and between her thighs.

Helen arched up to his mouth, gave him easy access, all the while wanting to pleasure him in return. Tangling her fingers in his hair, she tugged at him so that he looked up. She could see his mouth kissed with a slick wetness.

"What?" he whispered.

In answer, she tugged at him until he moved forward. Then she kept him moving until he lifted himself over her and she could grasp his cock and guide it to her mouth.

Her tongue met his tip and licked the drop of precome, then burrowed along the tiny slit. His groan spurred her on to give him more pleasure. She rimmed him and took him in her mouth, drawing on the soft fleshy tip until it slid deep into her mouth.

"Oh, darlin', yes," he gasped, pushing farther inside.

Then he set a rhythm, slow and sensuous, as he slid out and back in. Her hands found his buttocks and held him from escaping her completely.

Still moving, he groaned. "I want...let me...inside you..."

But she wouldn't release him. Instead she seduced him with her teeth...her tongue...her fingers. She cupped his balls and gently rolled them together, then circled the base of his cock and squeezed hard. She felt the flesh inside her mouth respond.

But before he could come, he forced himself back from her, murmuring, "Together."

He trailed his tip down between her breasts and over her stomach until it nestled at her entrance, hot and wet and ready for him. And as he kissed her, she opened wide and he slid inside, the creamy connection making a soft sucking sound that wrenched a gasp from her. He released her mouth and pushed himself up with straight arms on either side of her shoulders and began to move inside her. Sensation spread all the way to her fingers and toes. She wrapped her legs around his thighs and tightened herself inside.

Surely he would come now.

But he kept his movements lazy—slow and controlled. Her tilted hips drove him deeper. Her arched back allowed her to rub her breasts against his chest. No matter the stimulus, he took his time with her.

"You want me to come?" he whispered, nipping her earlobe. "Then help me."

"Whatever you want."

"I want to see it on your face. I want to watch as you come with me. Your clit." He lifted his lower body from hers slightly. "You do it…"

She lowered her legs and she could see him watch her hand disappear in between them. And then as her fingers found her juices and spread them over herself intimately, he watched her face as he'd said he would.

Heat flooded her, sort of an embarrassed pleasure.

"That's it." His eyes closed to slits. "More."

She set her feet on the bed for better access. He pulled out a bit and she moved in her hand so that she could touch both herself and him.

He stroked her with the same rhythm she used to stroke herself. Every time she was close to coming, she slowed—and then he slowed, further drawing out the pleasure. His face grew as taut as the muscles of his arms, still straight on either side of her shoulders. Forcing him in deeper, she quickened her strokes, and he followed suit.

A quaking began deep inside, then spread like lightning to her extremities. She gasped and tried to hold herself back. She wanted more.

But when he urged, "That's it, come for me, darlin'," she did.

Great waves of sexual current engulfed her, their intensity heightened by his war cry as he came right along with her for the shocking ride. Somehow he stayed hard enough to draw out her orgasm, giving her a second, prolonged climax.

Then he fell to the mattress beside her. They were both breathing hard, their bodies slicked with sweat.

Luke's hand found hers and their fingers laced together.

"I don't intend on sleeping tonight," he told her. "I don't want to waste a minute with you. I just thought you ought to know that."

"Bring it on," Helen challenged him. "I can take whatever you have."

He brought it on, making her come twice more before he himself could fully join in. Then he took her lying down...standing...up against the wall in the shower.

But even Luke DeVries was human. No matter his determination, his will wasn't as strong as the need for his body for rest. Somewhere in the wee hours of the morning, his conscious mind gave way while his body remained cocooned around hers.

Content for the moment, Helen relaxed against him and refused to think about the morning.

DAWN WAS SPILLING through the bedroom windows when Luke awakened. Feeling empty, he turned in his king-size bed to seek the comfort of Helen's body pressed against him.

She wasn't there.

He sat up and, bleary-eyed, focused on the specter moving around the gray room, stopping in front of the mirror to poke at her wild honey hair.

She was fully dressed.

Filled with a sense of loss he wasn't ready to face, Luke said, "Hey, darlin', what's the hurry?"

"City inspectors."

"Not this early."

"I have to go home and change. And then I want to get to the café and go over every inch with a fine-tooth comb. I'm afraid if I don't they'll find something not to their liking."

Swinging his legs over the bed, he said, "I'll come with you and help."

"No, really."

She was holding out a hand, as if that could stay him. As if that could protect her from him. Something inside him tightened. Ignoring her protest, he rose and pulled on his briefs.

"If this happened because of me, I owe you."

"You don't owe me anything, Luke. You've been nothing if not generous and caring."

"Why does this sound like a goodbye speech?"

"Not goodbye. I'm sure we'll see each other around."

"See each other around?" he echoed, picking up his clothes from the floor where he'd left them and throwing them onto the bed. Even though he instinctually *knew,* he wasn't going to believe it until he heard it from her own mouth. He climbed into his trousers. "Damn those rules of yours!"

"It's better this way," she insisted, darting out of the room and crossing the living room as if the hounds of hell were on her heels. "You'll be leaving for New York soon, and—"

Following, he cut her off. "That hasn't been decided."

"Where doesn't matter."

As she escaped his apartment, he could see that it didn't. Still, he followed her straight to the elevator; and when it opened on demand, he got inside with her. He could tell her mind was made up, that she didn't want him to change it. Still, he had to try.

"You're really okay with this?"

"I have to be."

"You have to pay taxes," he said as they spilled out of the elevator, across the lobby and outside the front door. "You don't have to end a relationship before it gets off the ground! Why don't you give us a chance?"

Already on the sidewalk, she turned to him and he could see the torn expression cross her face as she asked, "A chance to what?"

"I don't know." He really didn't. He only knew that already—before she was physically gone—he was mourning the loss of her. "I've never done this before."

"Neither have I. At least not for a long, long time. I still remember how much it hurt to be used and—"

"You think I'm using you?"

"I didn't say that."

"After everything that's happened, you believe Flash over me?"

"I believe that you're a great guy, Luke, but you

don't have a sense of permanence. You don't have a place to call home or longtime friends or—"

"Then teach me."

She shook her head and backed off. "I can't."

"Why not?" he demanded, but she was already racing down the street, as if afraid he would catch her and change her mind.

He let her leave. Watched her put distance between them. But he couldn't accept it.

Wouldn't accept it.

He let her leave, but he wasn't going to let her go.

THEIR ARGUMENT took away her breath.

Stepping out of the shelter of a tree, she watched a shirtless, shoeless Luke turn in frustration and reenter his building.

Then it struck her like a death knoll.

Maybe Luke DeVries mistakenly thought he was in love this time.

Bad enough that he didn't give her credit for all she'd done for him...that he'd never once taken her in his arms and kissed her mindless with his appreciation.

Bad enough that he'd held countless other women in his arms over the years but had never turned to her, the one woman who'd cared for him. Had made a success of him. Had committed crimes for him.

Now this.

How could he?

Swallowing hard, she felt her anger transfer from the woman...*to him.*

She watched his windows for what seemed like eons until he stepped out onto the metal balcony, his gaze pinned in the direction Helen had taken.

Even now the bastard was watching for the slut!

It was at that moment she knew all her love and loyalty had been for naught. At that moment she realized how thoroughly he had betrayed her.

She couldn't let him get away with it.

Never again.

14

"HOW FAR WOULD YOU GO to get what you want?" Luke asked Flash when she entered the office the next morning.

He himself had been there practically since Helen had walked out on him. Sleep had been impossible and he hadn't had an appetite, so he'd come here to throw himself into work.

As Flash searched through a file drawer, she said, "I don't give myself limits."

"Never?"

She glanced up. "You make that sound like a bad thing."

"It can be if you hurt someone else."

"In my business, feelings are subjective."

"Actually, I didn't mean feelings," Luke said, her statement reminding him of Helen.

He knew she had feelings of some kind for him, so why was she being so stubborn with those damn rules of hers? What was it going to take to get her to bend?

"I meant something more tangible," he went on. "Like another business. Or the person who owns it."

Drawing herself up to her considerable height,

Flash asked, ''Are you accusing me of something?'' Her voice held a touch of iciness.

''Not at all. I'm simply having a conversation with you. Suggesting some parameters. I play a straight game and expect my employees to do the same.''

He'd hoped coming at her sideways would be more effective than a head-on strike. He didn't expect a confession, but he'd hoped he could stop any more attacks on Helen's business. Or on the woman herself.

''I consider myself warned. Is that all?''

''One more thing—which business?'' he prodded.

''What?''

''Which did you mean by 'my business'—public relations or Hot Zone?''

''Luke, what is this all about?''

''You're heavily invested in Hot Zone, Flash. Sometimes I think even more than I am, and that's saying a lot.''

''Considering that it moves us from one city to another, takes the place of home and hearth and family and friends, it would be difficult to stay detached—''

Suddenly Luke realized that the way he ran his company hadn't only affected himself but Flash and Alexis, as well. He'd taken from them what his father's military career had taken from him.

''—but I'll get over it,'' Flash finished.

''That kind of sounds like a resignation.''

''Not yet, but I'm working on it.''

How long had he been asleep on the job? Luke wondered. If his employees were unhappy, he should know about it. He should know about a lot of things....

He said, "Not that I blame you for trying to better your professional status, but why now?"

"Let's just say that, despite my best efforts, I'm not where I'd planned to be at this point in my life."

And where exactly might that be? Luke wondered. Not that he had a chance to ask.

She'd already left the room.

HELEN WAS RELIEVED by her café's clean bill of health if not by the fine accompanying the violation. Certain that she'd been set up, she would love to shove the bill in the guilty party's face, if only she knew who that might be. Maybe the culpable one was trying to nickel and dime her until she was forced into closing her doors.

Helen tried to concentrate on the positive.

The café was open again. Customers came in and out at a steady if not breathtaking pace. Kate had shown up within a half hour of Helen's call.

Too bad this cloud of doom still hung over her head.

She delivered a fresh cup of coffee to Nick where he was checking his e-mail at one of the computer stations.

"What's with the gloom and doom?" he asked, frowning when he got a look at her face.

"I don't know what's wrong with me," she admitted. She was angry over someone trying to kill business for her, but that wasn't it. "I *am* happy that my doors are still open."

"The big *L*," Nick said. "It's as simple as that."

"Love is never simple."

"When Cupid aims that arrow—"

"But I ducked."

"Apparently not soon enough."

Helen grunted at him and cleaned off a few tables. The only regular around was Tilda. The old homeless woman was sitting at the window, reading a newspaper someone had left earlier. Surprising that she'd come back after her near-hysteria the other day.

Helen could only hope things would get back to normal in all respects over the next day or two. Or as normal as they could get considering someone was trying to ruin her.

That was where the gloom and doom came from. Not that she was about to argue with Nick, who became fixated on his ideas and would torture her if she tried to tell him otherwise.

But when she saw Luke come in halfway through the morning, Helen felt as if her heart had slammed up against her ribs. And felt as if a big bubble that had been welling inside her had burst at last.

Despite the reaction, she tried to act casual. "The usual?"

"I'd love the usual, but I'll settle for a Breve. Maybe—Kate, is it?—" he said without taking his eyes off Helen, "can make it while we talk." He indicated one of the tables away from everyone.

Knowing arguing would be useless, fearing he

would make a scene if she didn't go along with his plan, Helen said, "Fine. Kate, would you make Luke a Breve?"

"I'm on it."

When Helen sat with Luke, she tried steering the conversation away from the personal. "Did you have that talk with your employees?"

"Only Flash. I haven't seen Alexis yet this morning."

"Well?"

"Nothing concrete. But I warned her."

"I guess that's all I can expect," Helen said, standing.

Luke grasped her wrist. "You can expect a lot more from me, Helen, and I won't disappoint you. At least, I'll do my best not to."

"Good. I can always use a friend."

"I'm not interested in being just a friend. Sit, please."

Reluctantly doing as he asked, she glanced at the door when the bell signaled a customer. Alexis.

She headed straight over and dropped a cell phone onto the table in front of Luke. "You left this at the Hot Zone. I thought you might need it." She didn't spare Helen a glance.

"Thanks, Alexis," Luke said to her retreating figure as he stuffed the phone in his pocket.

"Now's your chance to talk to her," Helen said quietly.

"I'll talk to her later in private. I would like to talk to *you* in private—"

"I don't think so."

"Why not?"

"I thought you understood."

"I understand some creeps gave you a hard time and hurt you. I'm not one of them. And it isn't fair of you to put me in the same category."

"I don't. This isn't about you—"

"The hell it isn't! You feel something for me and it scares you." The outside door opened again, but Luke wouldn't be distracted. "It scares me, too, but I'm willing to chance anything for us to be together."

Helen's heart thumped and her stomach twisted into a knot. But before she could respond, Flash was at their table, waving something in the air.

"Clippings about the opening," she said, setting down a folder in front of Luke.

"Good press?"

"Great press. And there's more. A live radio interview." She checked her watch. "In fifteen minutes."

Reprieve! Helen rose.

A paper cup in each hand, Alexis stopped at the table. "Apparently this is yours," she said, setting one down in front of her boss.

"No time for a coffee break," Flash said. "You'll have to bring it with you."

"Hang on a minute!" Luke moved fast enough to catch up to Helen as she tried in vain for a clean getaway. "Can I see you tonight?"

"Busy."

"After hours."

"I'm spending time with my mother." Something she'd actually been thinking about doing.

"Late, then."

She shook her head. "I don't think so."

"Luke!" Flash called. "Twelve minutes till air time!"

Reluctantly, he backed off. "This isn't finished." Helen didn't respond and Luke started for the door, saying, "Okay, let's go."

Alexis had already left, but Flash was there, holding his drink out to him. "Wait, your coffee."

"I don't want it anymore."

"But you paid for it," she insisted.

"Actually, I didn't." Luke threw a five-dollar bill at Kate. "Just leave it," he said, before storming out the door.

Appearing frustrated, Flash set the paper cup back on the table and went after him.

"He was certainly rude," Kate said, ringing up the sale.

"He has a lot on his mind."

"I'll just bet he does."

Helen tried not to let Kate's mood affect her but found she could get dark and broody all on her own. Keeping busy until the noon rush started would be a good idea. And the Muscle Beach Web site was just the ticket to zone out of her own troubles and zero in on something positive.

Kate approached the table where Helen had been sitting with Luke. "I thought they left the drink," she muttered.

Indeed, the table was clear as were the others. The only paper cup in sight was the one in Tilda's hand. Kate whipped the wet rag over the surface and Helen went to work.

Working did help her mood. And while adding the list of links, Helen stumbled on a couple of Web sites using Java that caught her interest. She bookmarked anything she thought she could use later as a model. And her sense of accomplishment at finally finishing the Web site—a first draft, anyway—made her feel more in control.

Until a long, low moan sent a ripple of unease up her spine. She turned to see what was going on. Tilda was clutching her stomach, trying to get out of her chair.

"Tilda? Are you all right?" Helen asked, scraping back her chair and hurrying over to the old woman, who was now clinging to the table for support.

"S-si-ick."

Figuring Tilda was trying to get to the rest room, Helen took her arm. "Let me help you."

"Dizzy," Tilda said with a gasp.

She'd grown pale and her face shimmered with perspiration. Helen feared she was having a heart attack.

"Call 9-1-1," she told Kate over the old woman's protests.

Tilda wouldn't let Helen into the rest room with her, but Helen didn't move an inch from the door. She steeled herself against the sounds of the woman being sick and wondered what she could do to help until the paramedics arrived.

"Tilda, are you okay?" she asked.

The answer was a loud thunk, as if the woman had fallen.

"The ambulance is pulling up to the curb," Kate said.

Pulse racing, Helen was already fumbling with her keys, unlocking the door. *Dear Lord, please don't let her be dead!*

"That way," she heard Kate say, and even as she got the door open, two paramedics were at her side.

Tilda lay on the floor, shaking.

"Seizure," one of the paramedics said, scrambling to get inside.

Gasping, Helen stepped back and let them work. The next twenty minutes went by in a haze. Then, once again, Helen left the café in Kate's hands as she followed the ambulance to the hospital.

The wait seemed interminable, but eventually a woman who looked younger than Helen but wore a tag that identified her as a doctor came to find her.

"Did she make it?" Helen asked.

"She'll be all right. We're going to keep her overnight. Do you know anything about her family?"

"I don't even know if she has one."

Helen suspected she was the closest thing Tilda had to family, the café the closest thing to a home for the poor woman. She explained the situation to the young doctor, who appeared disturbed.

"What aren't you telling me?" Helen asked.

"It wasn't her heart—she was poisoned. I'm sure the police will want to talk to you."

"Poisoned?" a horrified Helen repeated. "But she didn't eat anything at the café today."

"Did she drink anything?"

"Just coffee." Her coffee was poisoned? "What kind of poison?"

"We'll know for certain when we have the test results, but from collective experience...we all think it might have been tetrahydrozoline, the active ingredient in some brands of eye drops and nose sprays."

"You think someone put eye drops in her coffee?"

"As I said, we've seen that kind of poisoning before—usually a gang member who got his buddies angry and they punish him by making him sick. The problem is, sometimes it actually kills them. Luckily, you called the paramedics in time."

Helen could hardly take it all in. "But...no gang members come into the café."

Suddenly panicked, she had to do something. She couldn't let this happen to anyone else. Wanting in the worst way to call Luke, she decided she needed to handle this one on her own and called Kate instead.

"How is Tilda?" Kate asked. "She isn't dead, is she?"

"No, she came through it. They're keeping her for observation till morning."

Then what? Helen wondered. Where would poor Tilda go?

"Thank God," Kate said.

"Has anyone else gotten sick?" Helen asked her.

"No, at least not as far as I know."

Helen breathed a sigh of relief. "Don't serve anyone else and close up shop."

"What? Again?"

"I'm sorry, Kate, but I don't know what else to do."

"I don't understand."

"I don't want anyone eating or drinking anything in the café until we know for certain what happened to Tilda."

She didn't want to go into it further. She didn't need to start spreading rumors about her own establishment that might be unfounded.

Still, when the police arrived and took her statement, then interrogated her, Helen felt guilty—as if she could have prevented this somehow. And when word came that the docs had diagnosed the poisoning correctly, the cops agreed that someone from forensics needed to check out the café, just in case. They were obviously concerned that other people might be affected, as well.

After visiting Tilda and promising she would make sure her possessions were safe, Helen headed back to the café with a growing sense of doom she couldn't shake.

HELEN HAD barely stepped out of the elevator before her mother opened the door to her apartment.

"Honey, what's wrong?"

"Everything, Mom."

She walked straight into her mother's waiting arms.

But for once the fierce hug didn't give her the expected result. She fought tears.

"Let's go inside. Did you eat?"

"I'm not hungry."

"That's not what I asked." Her mother led her straight to the pristine white kitchen and indicated a stool at the breakfast counter. "Sit."

"Mo-o-om."

"Don't 'Mom' me. Tell me what brought you here."

While her mother busied herself putting a pot on the stove and rummaging in a cabinet for a can, Helen told her about the crazy things going on at the café, including that day's near miss. And even though professionals had gone over her café, they hadn't found anything to prove that Tilda had gotten sick there. Only Helen was certain that she had.

"I have the awful feeling that it's part of someone's plan to ruin me. But this time it's serious. Someone could have died. If we'd actually found proof, the police would remain involved. Then there'd be an official investigation. As it is, I feel... vulnerable...like a sitting duck."

"Oh, sweetheart, that's terrible. No wonder you're so upset."

Her mother concentrated on the pot on the stove, giving Helen time to think—as if that wasn't all she'd been doing since this happened.

Why Tilda? Because she was disposable, because no one would miss or raise a fuss over a homeless woman? Helen shuddered and tried to remember when exactly Tilda had gotten a refill of coffee.

"Have some soup," her mother said, interrupting her thoughts.

"Chicken soup won't make everything better."

"No, but maybe it'll help."

Helen knew her mother would nag her until she put something in her stomach, so she took a spoonful of soup. Then another. She thought more about Tilda but couldn't remember her getting a refill anytime close to when she'd gotten sick. But she had been drinking from a paper cup...

Helen realized the soup was gone.

"Better?" her mother asked.

"I'm not shaking inside anymore."

"Well, then, it's a start. Somehow, I don't believe the café is your only worry. So what's on your mind?"

"I told you."

"You said 'everything' was wrong, so what else?"

Unable to meet her mother's gaze, Helen caved. "All right. It's Luke."

"What did he do?"

"Only everything I wanted."

"And then he left you?"

"No, I ended it. And he won't let me. He says I'm being unfair to him."

"Are you?"

"Not in my opinion. I told him about my three-date rule at the start."

Her mother started. ''Pardon me? You mean as in three strikes and he's out.''

''That's the gist of it,'' Helen said, unwilling to explain the exact parameters.

''I'm sorry, sweetheart, but I don't understand. Why in the world would you have some arbitrary rules about dating?''

''Because of you.''

''Oh, no, you can't blame this one on me.''

''Not blame, Mom. It's not your fault.'' They'd never had an honest conversation on the subject before, and Helen figured there was no use in making her mother feel as terrible as she did. ''No,'' she said, jumping off the stool, ''I can't talk about this, after all.''

''Helen Marie Rhodes, you will not leave here until we do talk about it.''

Helen never had been able to defy her mother when she used that tone. ''I never wanted to hurt your feelings.''

''You won't.''

Stubborn expressions ran in the Rhodes family. Helen knew when she was beaten.

''It's just that I never wanted to end up like you, Mom—unmarried and brokenhearted.''

Her mother choked back a laugh. ''Wherever did you get that idea? I'm the one who didn't want to marry.''

''But you loved my father. Didn't you?''

''At the time, yes. But I saw what life was like for my mother and older sister who both married too young and had too many kids and no life outside their homes. I didn't want that for myself. I don't even remember when I made the decision to stay single."

"But you got pregnant."

"Yes, I was blessed with you. Sometimes the unexpected happens. Being a single parent was my choice."

"I always thought Father left you when you told him you were pregnant with me."

"Oh, honey, I knew we should have had this talk years ago. I tried to bring it up so many times, but you always changed the subject."

"I didn't want you to be sad."

"I'm not sad. And I didn't exactly tell your father about the pregnancy, either. At least not right away. I broke up with him instead. He married on the rebound, and when he learned the truth, he was very angry with me. But what was the difference? I never would have married him. And I counted myself blessed to have you to look after. You were all I ever needed as someone permanent in my life. The only thing I'm really sorry about is that he couldn't make room for you. He said it was too painful, that you were a reminder of all he'd lost."

Helen was stunned. "So he rejected me and set up a trust fund to soothe his conscience?"

"That's very harsh, Helen."

"That part of my life *has* been harsh, Mom. There were times when I could have used a real dad, even if he didn't live with us."

Experience had set her up to distrust men from an

early age. And in the case of her father, she'd been right. He'd shut her out of his life to protect himself. What a crappy thing to do to a kid! If he'd known about the pregnancy before he'd married on the rebound, what then? Helen sighed. Her mother wouldn't have married him and it probably wouldn't have made any difference to her anyway.

"I'm so sorry you've been hurt, sweetheart."

"Me, too," Helen said. "All these years, I thought you and I were so much alike—trophy women for guys who only wanted us for the thrill."

"It seems we are alike," her mother said, "if in a very different way than you imagined. We've both driven away the men we loved and who loved us."

Helen quickly said, "I didn't say anything about love," but her pulse rushed through her and her mouth went dry at the denial.

"You didn't have to." Her mother stroked her cheek. "I can see it on your beautiful face. Does Luke feel the same?"

"I—I don't know."

"Then maybe you'd better find out."

Maybe she had. And maybe she'd better figure out exactly what it was she felt for him.

Helen rose and hugged her mother tight. "How come you're so smart?"

"Duh…I'm your mother."

15

LEAVING HER MOTHER'S APARTMENT around Hot Zone's closing time, Helen took a chance that Luke would still be there. She thought to call him first, then changed her mind. Now anxious to see him, she felt as if the taxi ride took forever. Certainly enough time for her to think.

And admit that she didn't really want to end it with Luke, after all.

If a better man was out there for her, Helen couldn't fathom who he might be. Luke respected her, understood her, wanted her. He made her heart race and her pulse zing. She looked forward to their every encounter, and when they weren't together, she found herself thinking about him.

So what was she going to do about it?

Even if she capitulated, Luke's business kept him on the move. What kind of a relationship could she have with a man who never lived in one place for more than a few months at a time?

She'd told him that he wasn't right for her because he had no place to call home, no longtime friends. She now remembered that he'd asked her to teach him.

Teach him?

Could she?

Her nerves trilled as she alighted from the taxi in front of Hot Zone. Several people were just leaving the building and Alexis was locking the door behind them. Helen rushed forward and waved to get the young woman's attention. Alexis started, then stood there glowering for a moment before unlocking the door to let Helen in.

"We *are* closed."

"I'm not here for coffee. I need to see Luke."

"Big surprise."

Suddenly Helen got an image—Alexis at the cybercafé carrying two cups and handing one to Luke. Now why had she thought of that?

Heart thumping, she suddenly had a flash....

"I need to tell him why I had to close shop early again. A woman almost died."

"What?"

"Tilda, the poor old homeless woman." She closely watched Alexis's face for any telltale sign of guilt. "It seems she drank coffee laced with the active ingredient found in eye drops and nose sprays. By the time the paramedics arrived, she was having a seizure."

"But she's okay?"

"She's still in the hospital," Helen said, trying to read Alexis without success.

"Well, that's good at least. Luke's in there," the young woman mumbled, heading for the stairs.

Was Alexis the guilty one? Helen wondered, now doubly anxious to see Luke.

He was talking to a couple of his new employees, so she hung back near the foyer and waited until they left, heading for the back door. Luke had started turning off lights before he spotted her. His expression didn't change as he crossed the floor and met her halfway.

"We need to talk," they both said at once.

"Me, first," Helen added. Though she was now focused on the poison attempt rather than anything more personal. "But I don't want to be overheard."

"Everyone's gone."

She shook her head. "Alexis just ran upstairs."

"Probably to get her things. You look flushed. Let me get you something cold to drink."

She said, "Thanks," before realizing Luke meant to fix them frozen coffees.

As he prepared the blender, she said, "You don't need to do anything fancy."

"I know I don't. But I want to."

His idea of seduction? Helen wondered, unable to summon a smile. She couldn't work up any enthusiasm for fancy coffees tonight.

So while he concocted, she paced and watched the stairs. Eventually Alexis descended, bag in hand. Luke's assistant stopped and stared their way for a moment, then, back stiff, she hurried toward the back door herself. She didn't even call out a good-night.

Helen was trying to decide if her behavior was suspicious or simply normal for a young woman with an unrequited crush when Luke said, "Come sit."

He placed the drinks on the table in the middle of a cozy seating area and made himself comfortable on the couch. Helen joined him but, as she took a long sip of her drink, she couldn't relax.

"It's good," she admitted, knowing he would expect her to analyze the ingredients. "Caramel... chocolate..." Another sip. "Toasted pecan?"

"You nailed it. It's something new I've been working on. A Frozen Turtle."

"Not a very *hot* name."

"If you have any ideas, don't be shy."

The double meaning sent a sizzle through her, but Helen ignored her reaction. "I didn't stop by to talk about fancy drinks."

"So what *is* on your mind?"

"I had to close up the café early again."

Luke started. "What now?"

"You know the homeless woman Tilda who's always around? She was poisoned today."

Helen told him about the trip to the hospital and the useless follow-up inspection of the café.

Luke shook his head. "Who would want to hurt a harmless old woman?"

"No one." She took a big breath before saying, "I think someone wanted to hurt *you.*"

"Uh...you just lost me."

"I poured Tilda's coffee myself this morning...into a *mug.* And right before she got sick, she was drinking out of a *paper cup.*"

"So?"

"You didn't take your Breve with you. Flash left it on the table, but then it disappeared. Tilda has a habit of collecting things other people leave behind—usually abandoned newspapers or food someone didn't finish. But this time I think it was your coffee."

"And you think it was laced with something dangerous. You're serious."

"Dead serious. If enough of that stuff had been in the coffee, she might have died. Or if you'd taken it with you, *you* could have died. At the very least you would have been horribly sick like she was."

"But there's no proof, right?"

Helen shook her head. "I'm afraid not. There wasn't any trace of the stuff at the café. Kate must have cleaned up Tilda's table and then dumped a bag of garbage before closing up. The cup would have been in it. But I didn't think about that or your missing cup until later, when I was at my mother's apartment. Then it hit me..."

Luke sat back and took it all in, and it was obvious he couldn't quite wrap his mind around this newest twist. Helen could hardly blame him. A loyal employee committing crimes in his name was pretty mind-boggling.

"You mentioned Alexis bringing me the Breve," he mused. "You're saying you think she tried to kill me?"

"Kill? I don't exactly believe that. More like make you sick and make me look bad at the same time. If the media gets hold of this..." Helen took a big breath. ''Anyway, if the paramedics hadn't gotten to Tilda in time, she would be dead now. Think about it, Luke. A bottle of drops is small. Alexis could have done a little sleight of hand right there at the counter when Kate wasn't looking. And you should have seen Alexis's reaction to me when I showed up tonight. She hates the fact that we're together—''

''We're together? Really?''

Helen pushed past the personal note. ''She was probably angry and wanted to get back at you.''

''Whoa. Let's go back a step to the together part,'' Luke insisted.

''You're not taking me seriously.''

''Of course I am. I always take you seriously.''

''Then what are we going to do?''

''I've already done something,'' Luke told her. ''I was thinking about your woman-behind-the-man theory and decided to call in a private investigator.''

''To check out Alexis?''

''And Flash.''

''Why didn't you tell me?''

''I only made the connection this morning and didn't have a chance. Suddenly Flash was there in the café telling me I had to go right then.''

And another image niggled at Helen.

''Flash...she was holding your coffee, too.'' Helen could picture the public relations woman standing at the table, waving the paper cup at him. ''Remember? She was trying to get you to take it.''

From his expression, Helen knew Luke did remember.

"So if your theory is true," he said, "not only is one of them ruining the competition wherever we go, but she also tried to slip me a mickey. Nice."

"One of them tried to hurt you because of me." A conclusion Helen had drawn and couldn't ignore. "In the past it was just the business. But there was the stair incident the other night...and now this."

Luke moved in on her and lifted her chin. His touch took away her breath.

"You're not to blame for anything here, Helen."

"And neither are you," she said. "And I'm sorry I ever distrusted you or agreed to that first date just to get information from you."

"You were playing with my feelings?"

"I'm sorry—I was conditioned to be suspicious of men's motives," Helen said before realizing he was putting her on. She narrowed her gaze at him. "Besides, you only wanted to date me to neutralize me, so that I wouldn't hurt your opening with another picket line."

"So we both had ulterior motives."

"At first," she admitted.

"And then?"

"And then your charm wore me down."

"Wow, what brought on all this honesty?"

"A talk with my mother," Helen admitted. "A very wise woman. She straightened me out on some misconceptions I've been carrying around since... well, forever. She made me see that I..."

"What?"

Unwilling to commit herself further with Luke

probably leaving for The Big Apple in the too-near future, she said, "If you still want, I'll agree to another date with you."

Even that simple admission made her throat tighten and her breath catch there. At last Luke smiled, the dimple in his cheek winking at her, making Helen's stomach tumble and that breath come out in a big whoosh.

"It's a start," he said agreeably.

Before she could inform him that she was promising nothing further, his mouth was covering hers and it was too late to say anything at all.

As they always seemed to, Luke's kisses made her lose her head. She kissed him back and forgot everything else and surrendered to the needs, both physical and emotional, that no other man had ever made her face. She'd always been self-sufficient before, but even in this short week she'd learned to count on Luke.

Her count on a man? That was something she never thought she would do.

Wrapping her arms around his back, she pulled him closer. But no matter how she angled her body, she couldn't get close enough to suit her. As if he could sense her dissatisfaction, Luke adjusted their positions even as he continued kissing her. He pushed her down on the couch and settled over her. Sparks seemed to ignite everywhere their bodies touched.

Placing a hand in the middle of his chest, Helen pushed until Luke came up for air and pulled back slightly. "Something wrong?" he asked.

"I just want to clarify...this isn't the date I agreed to."

His eyebrows shot up. "Then you want to stop?" He started to rise.

Helen held him fast. "I didn't say that, now did I?" She simply wanted to make sure this wasn't the last time they would be together.

"In all dating or otherwise related situations, you're the boss."

Yeah, sure she was.

"Then kiss me again," she ordered.

Helen savored the taste of his mouth on hers. A treat she wouldn't be experiencing at the moment if only Luke hadn't left the coffee behind. The thought made the kiss all the sweeter. More emotional. Gut-wrenching, even.

What if he had been the one to drink it?

But Luke was unharmed. And he was hers, at least for now. And Helen was determined to take advantage of every second, so she put away her dark thoughts for the time being.

Her short skirt had tugged up, revealing lots of leg, and he took advantage, stroking her outer thigh with the tips of his fingers.

Pressing his forehead to hers, he murmured, "Are you wearing underwear tonight?"

Her flesh rippled in response. "Afraid so. You?"

"That's for you to find out."

Gladly, she unzipped his trousers and reached inside to find him. "Tease," she said, stroking him into steel-rod-hardness through his briefs.

A gratifying sound escaped him. "So, what are you going to do about it?"

Choosing to show rather than tell, Helen slid the briefs down in front and hooked them below his balls, which made his cock jut out at her.

In turn, he ran a hand over her thong panties and pushed aside the crotch.

She trailed her fingers up his length and felt the sensitive muscles spasm.

He dipped his fingers into her thick juices, spread the cream ever-so-slowly upward through her delicate lips and over her clit. Her whole body responded, breasts tightening, flesh quivering.

Opening wider, she lifted her hips. "More," she demanded into his ear before biting it.

"Yes, ma'am."

He continued to stroke her and the pressure built so fast that she gasped.

"Music to my ears, darlin'," he murmured.

His tip probing at her entrance gave her double the pleasure. She moaned in approval and lifted her hips higher to receive him.

Luke slid home like he belonged there, which Helen was starting to believe he did. She could think of no greater pleasure than driving him senseless every night with different ways of having sex.

Different ways of saying she loved him.

Her eyes flashed open at the forbidden thought. He was staring at her, drinking her in, as he continued to stroke with both cock and finger.

When she squeezed him tight inside, as though she

would never let him go, the pleasure multiplied to new heights and, try as she might, she couldn't hang on, so she went with the delicious flow. Wave after wave of orgasm spilled one over the other. She clutched at him, hung on for dear life, until he was spent.

Then they lay together, he still in her, kissing and sighing in content.

LUKE DEVRIES disgusted her. Having slipped in through the back door, she stood mere yards from their tangled bodies and spewed mental venom.

How could she ever have imagined she loved him?

Look at him, the prick, sprawled all over Helen Rhodes, the bitch in perpetual heat. So self-involved…so certain of their mortality…

But she could fix that.

Even as she thought how, she knew she'd sunk to a new low, one that would put an end to everything.

Not her fault…they'd driven her to this. She had to end the pain they'd put her in, and she could think of only one way to do so.

Finding the supply closet, she removed the tools of their destruction.

HELEN AWOKE and took her time staring at Luke. He was equally handsome whether awake or asleep, she thought. But then she loved him—*loved him!*—and so she might be just the tiniest bit prejudiced.

Even as she thought the taboo words, her chest

squeezed tight and her stomach knotted. Love really was the scariest thing she'd ever faced.

Wanting to look her best for him when he awoke, she slipped from the couch, grabbed her purse and headed for the ladies' locker room. Wondering what that smell was—someone nearby using a fireplace in summer?—she glanced around but saw nothing amiss, so went inside.

They were both still fully dressed. She'd never made love fully clothed before. She'd never done a lot of things she'd done with Luke.

Smiling at the thought of more surprises to come, she freshened up and poked around at her hair. No matter what she did, she still looked like a woman who'd just made love…hot, sweaty, passionate love.

Helen smiled and dug in her purse for her lipstick.

Her fingers hit paper—the printouts of the articles on Hot Zone openings and the one about Luke being fired. Removing them from her purse, she then unfolded them and gave them another once-over.

Helen found herself staring at the photos, her gaze going from one page to the next to the next.

"Which one of you is guilty?" she asked the stills of Alexis and Flash. And then she spotted something she hadn't noticed before. Another familiar-looking woman. She glanced over to the article about Luke's firing and thought she saw the same woman in the background. "It can't be…"

But it was!

She gripped the papers tighter, meaning to show her discovery to Luke, but the moment she opened the locker room doors, she dropped everything in horror.

Smoke rolled in over her, while flames danced over couches and a coffee station.

Hot Zone was on fire!

16

LUKE JERKED AWAKE coughing. Water was streaming down on him from the ceiling, but the wet air was thick and cloying with something else.

Smoke!

Fire!

He flew to his feet and then collided with the edge of the couch when smoke seared his lungs. He coughed long and hard. The sprinkler system had gone on, but the choking atmosphere had intensified.

The source of flames and smoke came from his left. A couch and a couple of upholstered chairs were on fire. And beyond them, the coffee station…

Suddenly it hit him. Where the hell was Helen?

Between coughs he called out, ''Helen!''

''Luke, here.''

He turned to the sound of her voice and through a spreading cloud of dark smoke spotted her standing in the locker room doorway, her purse and papers strewn around her feet. Appearing terrified and frozen to the spot, she obviously didn't know which way to go.

He had to get her out of there and fast.

If anything happened to her…

The thought made Luke sick inside and forced him to move. Still coughing, he grabbed a couple of small pillows from the couch, both soaked with sprinkler water, and used one to shield his face. When he got to Helen, he handed her the other and she did the same.

Taking her hand, he led her around the fire, which hadn't yet spread, and pulled her toward the back door. Both coughing from the smoke despite the protection, they stumbled into the alley.

Helen fell against the building's brick exterior and gasped, "Cell phone. Call 9-1-1."

Taking in fresh air and trying to get his cough under control, Luke was staring into the burning interior. "An alarm has already gone off at the station. The fire department should be on its way."

But he couldn't wait. He couldn't watch his business go up in smoke before his eyes without trying to stop it. The fire was still small, still contained. He had to do something before it spread.

Thinking quickly, he said, "I have to go back inside."

"Luke, no!" Helen grasped his wrist as if she would never let him go.

"I'll be all right." He took her in his arms to reassure her. She was shaking, and so was he. "There's a hose in the janitor's closet. I'm going to try to put out the fire."

Helen clung to him, crying, "No, please."

But after kissing her quickly, Luke said, "Stay

put!'' pulled away and ran back into the burning building to fight the fire himself.

ANXIOUSLY WAITING for the fire trucks to arrive, praying that Luke would come out safely, Helen felt a moment's shock when someone came up behind her and shoved her hard against the building.

Gasping, she whirled around to find Kate Malone glaring at her.

''You bitch!'' her assistant spat.

Helen might have been surprised, but before leaving the locker room, she'd had that long, clear look at the clippings in her purse. The clippings had revealed a familiar pale, thin woman in the background of the photos accompanying both the article about the Hot Zone opening and Luke's termination from Cooper Coffee Company. Articles she'd dropped when she'd seen the fire.

The fire that Kate must have started.

''It's been you all along,'' Helen said.

''Right under your own nose.''

''Why, Kate?''

''Because I fell in love with Luke DeVries the moment I met him.''

As had she, Helen thought. Though she didn't think this was the right moment to say so.

''Luke doesn't even know you, Kate.''

''Because of you! You've blinded him or he would be mine. I'm the secret of Luke's successes. He wouldn't be anywhere without me.''

The woman was delusional. And clever. Helen remembered Kate responding to her ad for a job just as work had started on the Hot Zone renovation. Kate must have planned to put her out of business from the first...as she must have done to other competitors over the past three years.

Anger getting the best of her, Helen said, "Luke never knew you existed, did he, Kate? Not even at Cooper Coffee Company. Is that where you first became obsessed with him?"

With fire engines sounding in the distance, Kate said, "Yeah, I worked at the coffee brokerage, but he never so much as noticed me, not even when I applied for the job as his assistant. He passed me over for someone flashier. But I was determined to prove myself. I helped him at Cooper, too, but he was fired anyway."

"You mean he was fired *because of you.*"

Kate's jaw tightened. "Whatever. And when he started his own business, I figured that I could earn his trust and love by helping him build a success."

"The woman behind the man," Helen murmured.

"He never even thanked me for all my hard work," Kate said, her voice petulant as if she really thought he should. "But knowing my day would come, I made it a point to stay in the background. Now is that day. Finally, he's going to see me for who I am."

The fire engines were out front now. Helen could hear the engines...the sound of voices...the shattering of glass. Her heart went out to Luke. His business was being destroyed before it got off the ground.

Luke. Where was he? Suddenly she realized how long he'd been in there.

"Now is the day you go to jail!" Helen told Kate before yelling, "Luke, please come out!"

A man was heading over from the building next door and Kate suddenly seemed to realize she might be caught. "I'm not going anywhere I don't want to be!"

Kate tried to duck away, but Helen caught onto her arm and held fast.

"Help me!" she called to the man, who was wearing a security guard's uniform. "She started the fire!" And when Kate clawed her and ripped free of her grip, Helen ran, too. "Don't let her get away!"

The man sprinted and caught the fleeing woman, and as hard as Kate fought him, she couldn't wrench herself free.

Helen turned back to the doorway. Curls of escaping smoke taunted her. Still no Luke.

Sick inside, she stood there for a moment, but knew she couldn't simply wait to find out what happened to him. There was no one back here in the alley but Kate and her captor.

And her.

Frantic to make sure Luke got out of the burning building alive, Helen picked up the pillow and set it back over her face, then slipped back inside, ignoring the calls of warning from the man outside with Kate. The smoke seared her eyes but she followed the trail made by the hose until she found Luke on the floor, overcome by the smoke.

Dear God, don't let him be dead!

Firefighters were entering the building from the street side and a pressurized hose sent a stream straight at the quickly spreading blaze. One of the men spotted her and ran to help her get Luke up off the floor and out into the alley where a small knot of observers gathered and a uniformed officer was cuffing Kate.

The fireman set Luke down on the alley floor and called for paramedics who were already on the scene.

"Luke, listen to me!" Helen said frantically as she got to her knees and bent over him. She grabbed his shoulder and shook him. "You have to wake up. Our date isn't over. As a matter of fact, I decided that we should have more dates. A whole series of dates! I'll make a list, okay?"

Luke coughed himself into consciousness and Helen couldn't help herself. She started to sob in relief.

Grinning weakly, he gasped, "I'm going to be just fine. And I'm going to hold you to that promise. What are you doing tomorrow night?"

AFTER A CHECKUP in the emergency room, Luke was released.

Before leaving the hospital, he and Helen talked to a detective, who took copious notes on the situation and on past situations that might also have been crimes committed by the woman who now called herself Kate Malone.

"I think her name was Sally something," Luke told

the detective. "She isn't the kind of woman who sticks in a man's memory."

The reason he'd never recognized her...and her reason for doing all those terrible things in the name of love.

Helen told the detective about the articles and photographs she'd found and promised she would get back online and make copies for him. The detective thanked her and promised to follow up with them in the morning.

Then Helen brought Luke home to take care of him.

He was still coughing, but otherwise seemed to be all right, so Helen was a little surprised when Luke asked her to help him upstairs and into the bathroom so he could shower off the grime from the fire. Thinking she needed to do the same, Helen hooked an arm around Luke's waist and guided him up the stairs.

"I still can't believe I hired that psycho," she said, despondent at the thought that she'd been so mistaken. "I always thought I was a pretty good judge of character. I even changed my mind about you once I met you."

They were in the bathroom now. Luke wrapped his arms around her and hugged her close.

"Some people are simply better actors than others," he said. "And Kate or Sally or whatever her name obviously has some kind of personality disorder. People with psychological problems can be very clever. Now help me get these clothes off, would you?" he asked in a tired voice.

Doing as he asked, trying to ignore the stirrings she felt with each touch, Helen said, ''If only I had figured out she was the one trying to sink me, you wouldn't be hurt and Hot Zone wouldn't have to be rebuilt.''

''There is a bright side to the situation,'' he said as his trousers slid down his legs to the floor.

''Bright side?'' she echoed.

''Having to rebuild will keep me here longer than either of us imagined. We'll have plenty of time for those dates you promised me.''

Suddenly Helen realized Luke was working on removing *her* clothes. Her response to the touch of his hands on her flesh was immediate and intense, but she couldn't simply give way to her feelings.

''About that...I was frantic at the time. I didn't know what I was saying.''

''You're trying to renege on our deal? C'mon, let's get in the shower.''

They were both naked now and both streaked with grime. Helen let him pull her to the shower stall, which was barely big enough for them both.

While he adjusted the water to a comfortable temperature, she said, ''I'm not trying to renege, I simply think we should take things one day at a time.''

He pulled her inside, under the spray of water, and closed the door, saying, ''So which day will you marry me?''

''What?''

''Marry me,'' he repeated, as if she hadn't heard him the first time.

Helen gaped at him. ''You're crazy—''

''True.''

''—we've only known each other for a week.''

''It feels like a lifetime to me,'' Luke said, moving in on her for a quick kiss. ''I've never had a place I wanted to call home before, but I want one now,'' he said, soaping her, his seductive strokes quickening her body, making her hazy-headed and weak-kneed. ''You've been friends with Nick and Annie forever. I want that with you. Hell, I want more. I want everything. The whole enchilada. A house. Kids. Everything. But mostly I want you. I want *you* to be the place I come home to.''

Words Helen had always longed to hear from a man she loved.

''Then come home now,'' she whispered, opening her arms to him and, more importantly, her heart.

Epilogue

LAST TO MEET, first to marry, and in a record month's time, at that. Helen turned to admire herself in the full-length mirror—because there hadn't been time for custom-made, her mom had insisted on choosing and buying the dress as a wedding gift. Mom should be here now, but earlier, she said she'd forgotten something and had rushed out in a tizzy.

"Wait until Luke sees you!" Annie said.

Isabel added, "You're a regular blond bombshell. He'll probably fall all over himself."

Thankful she'd put her trust in someone with more classic fashion sense than her own, Helen grinned at her reflection. The simple off-white satin clinging to her curves and just barely sweeping the floor behind her was something out of a thirties movie. Long gloves covered her arms over the elbows. To complete the look, she'd tamed her curls, and rather than a veil, had fastened in its strands a white magnolia like the ones in her simple bouquet.

"I can't believe this is happening," Helen said, nerves getting to her. "One of you pinch me!"

Annie snorted. "And have Luke asking where you got the bruise? I think not."

Helen hugged her best friend and maid of honor, beautiful in a slinky peach satin calf-length number. "You're next," she said, knowing Annie and Nate were planning a Christmas wedding. "And it won't be long before Nick pops the question," she said to Isabel, who was stunning in her lavender satin bridesmaid dress.

"I'm in no hurry," Isabel said. "But someday..."

Helen knew Isabel had barely gotten her career as a freelance political journalist off to a fine start, but she saw the way the other woman looked at Nick. And she knew Nick was more than ready. Maybe a spring wedding...

But now it was time for hers.

"Shall we?"

They left the dressing room of the church arm-in-arm only to run into her mom, who burst into tears at the sight of Helen.

"Mom, it's okay!"

"I know. It's more than okay," Christine Rhodes said, wiping at her eyes with one hand, holding out a jeweler's box with the other. "You're simply stunning."

Helen took the box. "What is it?"

"Something old."

The dress was new, the tiny thong and fancy garter belt Annie supplied blue, and Isabel had lent her a simple if stunning strand of pearls to wear. Helen opened the dark blue box and gasped when she saw the pearl and diamond bracelet lying across the inner velvet.

"It's beautiful. Mom, I've never seen this before. Where..." It hit her, then, why her mother wouldn't have shown it to her. "My father." Uneasy, she hesitated.

"We did love each other, Helen. He gave this to me when he asked me to marry him and he wouldn't take it back. Later, he told me that if you were a girl, I should give it to *you* on the day you married."

Knowing that to refuse would upset her mom, Helen held out her wrist. "You put it on me."

In an odd way, her father would be there through the bracelet. She'd invited him and her siblings, but they'd sent their regrets. Luke's kid sister Peggy, however, was in attendance with her mother and their father with his current wife. Alexis had brought her newly acquired boyfriend—apparently, she'd moved on emotionally now that Luke was spoken for. And Flash had moved on professionally, right out of town.

"Ready?" her mom asked.

Helen took a big breath. "As I'll ever be."

They all stepped into the garden where Nick took Isabel's arm and Nate took Annie's. The stringed trio began playing. A jittery Helen slipped her hand onto the arm of the woman who would give her away. Her mom patted her hand and Helen relaxed as they moved forward.

And when Luke saw her and his eyes widened and a smile lit his face, she lit up, too, from the inside out. Her mom gently pushed her toward him, and Helen let go of one life and stepped into a new one.

Luke took her hand and squeezed it, as if saying, *I'll never let you go.*

HARLEQUIN BLAZE COVER MODEL SEARCH CONTEST 3569 OFFICIAL RULES
NO PURCHASE NECESSARY TO ENTER

1. To enter, submit two (2) 4" x 6" photographs of a boyfriend or spouse (who must be 18 years of age or older) taken no later than three (3) months from the time of entry: a close-up, waist up, shirtless photograph; and a fully clothed, full-length photograph, then, tell us, in 100 words or fewer, why he should be a Harlequin Blaze cover model and how he is romantic. Your complete "entry" must include: (i) your essay, (ii) the Official Entry Form and Publicity Release Form printed below completed and signed by you (as "Entrant"), (iii) the photographs (with your hand-written name, address and phone number, and your model's name, address and phone number on the back of each photograph), and (iv) the Publicity Release Form and Photograph Representation Form printed below completed and signed by your model (as "Model"), and should be sent via first-class mail to either: Harlequin Blaze Cover Model Search Contest 3569, P.O. Box 9069, Buffalo, NY, 14269-9069, or Harlequin Blaze Cover Model Search Contest 3569, P.O. Box 637, Fort Erie, Ontario L2A 5X3. All submissions must be in English and be received no later than September 30, 2003. Limit: one entry per person, household or organization. **Purchase or acceptance of a product offer does not improve your chances of winning.** All entry requirements must be strictly adhered to for eligibility and to ensure fairness among entries.

2. Ten (10) Finalist submissions (photographs and essays) will be selected by a panel of judges consisting of members of the Harlequin editorial, marketing and public relations staff, as well as a representative from Elite Model Management (Toronto) Inc., based on the following criteria:

Aptness/Appropriateness of submitted photographs for a Harlequin Blaze cover—70%
Originality of Essay—20%
Sincerity of Essay—10%

In the event of a tie, duplicate finalists will be selected. The photographs submitted by finalists will be posted on the Harlequin website no later than November 15, 2003 (at www.blazecovermodel.com), and viewers may vote, in rank order, on their favorite(s) to assist in the panel of judges' final determination of the Grand Prize and Runner-up winning entries based on the above judging criteria. All decisions of the judges are final.

3. All entries become the property of Harlequin Enterprises Ltd. and none will be returned. Any entry may be used for future promotional purposes. Elite Model Management (Toronto) Inc. and/or its partners, subsidiaries and affiliates operating as "Elite Model Management" will have access to all entries including all personal information, and may contact any Entrant and/or Model in its sole discretion for their own business purposes. Harlequin and Elite Model Management (Toronto) Inc. are separate entities with no legal association or partnership whatsoever having no power to bind or obligate the other or create any expressed or implied obligation or responsibility on behalf of the other, such that Harlequin shall not be responsible in any way for any acts or omissions of Elite Model Management (Toronto) Inc. or its partners, subsidiaries and affiliates in connection with the Contest or otherwise and Elite Model Management shall not be responsible in any way for any acts or omissions of Harlequin or its partners, subsidiaries and affiliates in connection with the contest or otherwise.

4. All Entrants and Models must be residents of the U.S. or Canada, be 18 years of age or older, and have no prior criminal convictions. The contest is not open to any Model that is a professional model and/or actor in any capacity at the time of the entry. Contest void wherever prohibited by law; all applicable laws and regulations apply. Any litigation within the Province of Quebec regarding the conduct or organization of a publicity contest may be submitted to the Régie des alcools, des courses et des jeux for a ruling, and any litigation regarding the awarding of a prize may be submitted to the Régie only for the purpose of helping the parties reach a settlement. Employees and immediate family members of Harlequin Enterprises Ltd., D.L. Blair, Inc., Elite Model Management (Toronto) Inc. and their parents, affiliates, subsidiaries and all other agencies, entities and persons connected with the use, marketing or conduct of this Contest are not eligible to enter. Acceptance of any prize offered constitutes permission to use Entrants' and Models' names, essay submissions, photographs or other likenesses for the purposes of advertising, trade, publication and promotion on behalf of Harlequin Enterprises Ltd., its parent, affiliates, subsidiaries, assigns and other authorized entities involved in the judging and promotion of the contest without further compensation to any Entrant or Model, unless prohibited by law.

5. Finalists will be determined no later than October 30, 2003. Prize Winners will be determined no later than January 31, 2004. Grand Prize Winners (consisting of winning Entrant and Model) will be required to sign and return Affidavit of Eligibility/Release of Liability and Model Release forms within thirty (30) days of notification. Non-compliance with this requirement and within the specified time period will result in disqualification and an alternate will be selected. Any prize notification returned as undeliverable will result in the awarding of the prize to an alternate set of winners. All travelers (or parent/legal guardian of a minor) must execute the Affidavit of Eligibility/Release of Liability prior to ticketing and must possess required travel documents (e.g. valid photo ID) where applicable. Travel dates specified by Sponsor but no later than May 30, 2004.

6. Prizes: One (1) Grand Prize—the opportunity for the Model to appear on the cover of a paperback book from the Harlequin Blaze series, and a 3 day/2 night trip for two (Entrant and Model) to New York, NY for the photo shoot of Model which includes round-trip coach air transportation from the commercial airport nearest the winning Entrant's home to New York, NY, (or, in lieu of air transportation, $100 cash payable to Entrant and Model, if the winning Entrant's home is within 250 miles of New York, NY), hotel accommodations (double occupancy) at the Plaza Hotel and $500 cash spending money payable to Entrant and Model, (approximate prize value: $8,000), and one (1) Runner-up Prize of $200 cash payable to Entrant and Model for a romantic dinner for two (approximate prize value: $200). Prizes are valued in U.S. currency. Prizes consist of only those items listed as part of the prize. No substitution of prize(s) permitted by winners. All prizes are awarded jointly to the Entrant and Model of the winning entries, and are not severable - prizes and obligations may not be assigned or transferred. Any change to the Entrant and/or Model of the winning entries will result in disqualification and an alternate will be selected. Taxes on prize are the sole responsibility of winners. Any and all expenses and/or items not specifically described as part of the prize are the sole responsibility of winners. Harlequin Enterprises Ltd. and D.L. Blair, Inc., their parents, affiliates, and subsidiaries are not responsible for errors in printing of Contest entries and/or game pieces. No responsibility is assumed for lost, stolen, late, illegible, incomplete, inaccurate, non-delivered, postage due or misdirected mail or entries. In the event of printing or other errors which may result in unintended prize values or duplication of prizes, all affected game pieces or entries shall be null and void.

7. Winners will be notified by mail. For winners' list (available after March 31, 2004), send a self-addressed, stamped envelope to: Harlequin Blaze Cover Model Search Contest 3569 Winners, P.O. Box 4200, Blair, NE 68009-4200, or refer to the Harlequin website (at www.blazecovermodel.com).

Contest sponsored by Harlequin Enterprises Ltd., P.O. Box 9042, Buffalo, NY 14269-9042.

HBCVRMODEL2